DO UNTO OTHERS

Geonn Cannon

Supposed Crimes LLC • Matthews, North Carolina

ISBN: 978-1-952150-42-5

www.supposedcrimes.com

This book is typeset in Goudy Old Style.

Monday July 16, 1945

We were standing next to the truck when it happened. She stopped midsentence and looked over my shoulder.

"What in the world is that?"

Oldest trick in the book, right? Amateur. But neither of us was any amateur, and besides, I could see it in her eyes. Not just her expression, I mean, literally, I saw it in her eyes. Some kind of light, blooming, reflecting. So I looked over my shoulder. There was a line of light along the horizon, spreading out like spilled wine on a tablecloth.

"Sunrise," I said. It was about that time.

"That's south."

I turned around to face it fully. That's when we felt it. The ground under our shoes, shaking. Just a real low vibration, subtle enough that I wasn't entirely sure I felt it until I saw she was looking at her feet. By that time, the whole horizon had lit up. It would be months before we knew the truth. A test called Trinity. A new kind of horrible, awful weapon being exploded by a bunch of scientists somewhere about fifty miles south of us. The sun was still waiting to rise in its proper place. But to the south, it was bright as noontime, because a tiny little brand-new sun had floated up over the desert.

My heart was in my throat. I don't think I was breathing, and I wasn't sure if I'd stopped myself or if the air had all been burned away. That bright cloud just kept rising up and up and up, and then we heard it, like the sky cracking open. It knocked me back a step. I felt her hand on my shoulder, and then her other hand slipped into mine.

Despite everything, I gripped it tight. I think she needed it as much as I did. I barely even remembered what we'd been fighting about before the sky exploded.

What could it possibly have mattered at the end of the world?

Chapter One

NEW MEXICO
Monday July 9, 1945

The clouds started rolling in just after lunchtime. They filled up the formerly empty sky and the temperature sank in response. One two-lane road cut through the scrubland. The sun baked asphalt was barely distinguishable from the desert around it, forcing the lone vehicle on the road to straddle the middle lines so it didn't accidentally drift off the shoulder. It was a sturdy truck, forest green under a thick layer of dirt. The back was loaded with suitcases and boxes draped with a plain brown tarp that was anchored to the sidewalls.

The passenger side window of the truck was down so Penny Chaplin could smell rain on the air. She had long ago gotten bored by the landscape, unchanged by the past hundred miles or so. There were long stretches of desert scrub occasionally spiced up with broken-down fences and small farmhouses set far back from the main road. Sometimes there were bursts of green, but they were just oases that made the harshness around them more noticeable. The horizon was flat and unchanging save for the flat-topped hills that rose up here and there.

The rain would feel amazing after the past few days of driving in the hot truck. Penny was very fair, strawberry blonde and pale, and too much time in the sun made her feel like she was right on the verge of boiling. But Tinker was driving so it was her decision when and if the air conditioning could run. She almost always elected not.

Chaplin didn't understand why she'd paid so much for the feature if she was never going to use it, but Tinker was adamant. Her truck, her rules, and it wasn't worth arguing over. Chaplin just made certain her porkpie hat was secure and leaned closer to the window to catch the breeze.

Up ahead, she spotted a filling station. The sign advertised it as "SELF-SERVE ONLY." A truck was already parked on the building-side of the pumps. She glanced at Tinker, who acknowledged she'd also seen it without saying a word. The gas gauge wasn't a cause for alarm yet. It was only a few miles to the next town. But when they reached the small brick building, Tinker clicked on her turn signal and pulled off the road. She rolled to a stop on the other side of the pumps.

"Lend a hand?" Chaplin said.

"Watch my skills," Tinker said.

Chaplin nodded and got out of the truck. She crossed the patch of pavement in a few long strides. She undid the top few buttons of her shirt and fanned out the collar, perfectly reasonable given the temperature. She was in an emerald green blouse with suspenders and houndstooth pants. Not exactly an outfit designed for seduction of any sort, but she knew how to get blood from a stone. She adjusted her glasses, hooked her thumbs under her suspenders, and cleared her throat in anticipation of the speech she was about to give.

She swung open the door and was greeted by a beautifully cold blast. She looked gratefully up at the oscillating fan placed on top of a shelf near the cash register. She took a moment to appreciate the sweat drying on her face before she took in the rest of her surroundings.

A broomstick of a clerk - older, balding, more bone than beef - was casually resting his elbows on the counter. A customer, the driver of the other truck, leaned against the other side of the counter with a half-full bottle of Coke hanging from his hand. The other driver was barrel-thick and squat. They both turned and looked at her. She could sense the silence of a paused conversation.

"Afternoon, gentlemen!" she said, taking a step toward them with her first word. She gestured with her hands as she spoke. "You know what I miss? What I *genuinely* miss? Full-service gas stations. They used to be all over the place, but they're starting to become more rare, it seems. Now, I'm not casting aspersions on you, sir. Not at all. I know how much work you have on your hands running an establishment like this.

"But sometimes it's nice to be treated a little special. You know? You pull into a service station and a man in a tidy uniform runs out and cleans your windshield, checks your oil, kicks the tires, makes sure your carriage is in tip-top shape. It almost makes you feel like royalty, doesn't it? Just a little?"

The men exchanged amused looks. The customer nodded and stood up straighter. "I suppose you may have a point there, miss."

"Surely I do, surely. That's why my sister and I like to spread a little of that feeling around when we can. If you'd like, sir, she would be more than happy to wash your windows and make sure your car is in top working order."

They turned and looked outside. Tinker was waiting between the pumps. She smiled and lifted the squeegee in greeting.

"No charge," Chaplin added quickly. "We just like to spread a little joy around when it's in our ability to do so."

The customer laughed. "Why not. Go nuts."

Chaplin gave Tinker a thumbs-up. Tinker nodded and dipped the squeegee into the water.

While she got started on the windshield, Chaplin took the deck of cards from the back pocket of her trousers. She started shuffling them quick-like, with nimble and confident fingers.

"While she's doing that, gentlemen, how about we play a game?"

The clerk lifted his chin and smiled a knowing smile. "Ah, here we are. When the carny patter starts, it's only a matter of time before the game shows up."

"Just a game, sir, nothing carnival about it. In fact, if it sets your mind to ease, we won't even play for money. Just for fun, pride, and bragging rights." She flicked the cards from one hand to the other in a single wave. "What do you say, nothing lost but a few minutes of your day."

The customer chuckled and tapped the counter. "Let's see what you've got."

"I like you, sir, you seem like a very amenable fellow. Always going with the flow, seeing where the day takes you. It rarely takes us anywhere boring, if we're willing to go."

She shuffled while she spoke. She placed three cards face-up on the counter, seemingly at random, and returned the rest of the deck to her pocket. They were left with a King of Clubs, a Queen of Hearts, and a King of Diamonds. She knocked each card with a knuckle and named them.

"Meet Joe, Jane, and Jack. Jack's strong, he can flex and smile to get Jane on her back. But Joe's got dough, and you know how easily women are swayed by a man with coin. They're both after Jane's heart, but you can win it if you just keep her in your sights."

She flipped the cards over and used both hands to shift them.

"Get your girl, sir, find her or find out who stole her away. Jack's gonna come out swinging, Joe's got shiny rings and things, but the lady has your heart, and all you've gotta do is keep her from getting away. Are you watching, are you paying attention, are you following your heart, my friend?" She stopped shuffling them and moved her hands back. "Where's your lovely lass?"

The customer pointed to the center card. Chaplin hissed between her teeth and flipped it over to reveal the Queen.

"Glad we're not playing for money. How about you, sir?" She looked at the clerk. "Want to try your luck? Still just fun, nothing but fun."

"Why not."

She shuffled them again. "Your friend stole her heart, but there's still a chance she'll be swayed by a sharp-eyed clever man like you. A businessman, no less! What's not to love. But first you have to find her, and she's a quick'n, just when you think you've spotted her, she's nowhere to be found. Do you think you have what it takes to make her settle down?"

He touched the far right card. Chaplin flipped it over. Queen.

"You're excellent at the patter," the clerk said. "Maybe if you just get a little quicker with the cards."

"Maybe so, maybe so," she said, returning the cards to the deck. "I thank you for the opportunity to practice my skills."

She went to the icebox and came back with two bottles of Royal Crown. Before she could put them down on the counter, the customer waved her back.

"Put those on my tab, Bud."

Chaplin's eyes widened behind her glasses. "Are you sure? I don't want you feeling hustled here."

He shrugged, smiling wide. "Your sister washed my window and you provided a much needed bit of entertainment on an otherwise dull afternoon. It would be my pleasure. Besides, a gentleman always buys drinks for beautiful ladies."

She grinned. "Well, gosh. Thank you, sir."

"The name is Holland. James Holland. And I thank *you*, Miss..."

"Margaret Byrd, sir, lovely to meet you. And I'm sure my sister thanks you, too. It's been a real hot drive."

"I bet it has, young lady."

Chaplin looked out the front window. Tinker was putting the nozzle back on the gas pump. "Well, I still owe you for the gas. How much?"

The clerk, Bud, looked at the machine. "Looks like... forty-five cents."

He seemed to take note of the low price, but he didn't press it. Certainly a lot of people had come through and only gotten the bare minimum, just what they needed to get home. Chaplin put two quarters down on the counter and smiled to both men.

"Thanks again, gentlemen. And I'm going to get better at the game, promise."

"You do, then come on back and try your luck again," James Holland said. "Next time we may even raise the stakes a little."

Chaplin laughed softly. "Wow, exciting! Okay! Have a nice day, sirs."

She carried the bottles out to the truck. The engine was already running when she climbed into the passenger seat. Tinker pulled away from the pumps and got back on the main road. Chaplin used the bottle opener mounted on the dash to open their drinks and handed one of the bottles to Tinker. She took a long swig, swished it around in her mouth, and leaned to her left to spit it out the window.

"Get a mouthful again?"

"The fumes," Tinker said, wrinkling her nose. She took another drink. "Like kissing someone with gravestones as teeth."

"Blech."

Chaplin twisted to look in the back of the truck. A red jerry can was sitting against the sidewall, tucked in alongside their suitcases and other belongings.

While she distracted the truck's owner and the clerk, Tinker used the full-service routine to get the can from the bed of their truck. She'd slipped a hose out of her pocket. And under the pretense of checking the air pressure in the tires, knelt down and replaced James Holland's nozzle with her tube. Siphoning could literally leave a bad taste in Tinker's mouth, but hopefully the fizzy water in the pop would help wash it away.

"How much did we get?" she asked.

"A couple of gallons."

"Not bad. The pops were free, by the way."

Tinker grinned. "Did you charm the gentlemen, Miss Chaplin?"

"I didn't mean to," Chaplin said. "It just happens."

"Uh-huh." Tinker laughed. "Well, then. We came out better than I thought. We might have a nice fancy dinner tonight."

Chaplin whistled. "That would be swell."

They wouldn't stop in the next town. It was far too likely Holland was from there. It would definitely be one of the first places he'd go when he discovered his gas tank was nowhere near as full as it should be. He might blame the mechanism first, or crawl underneath to look for a leak, but eventually he would remember the lady who had been messing around with the truck at the filling station. It would be very good for them if they were long gone by the time he came looking.

As they left the filling station behind them, the sky opened up and began wetting the road with a nice, gentle shower. Chaplin left the window down and stuck her arm straight out, catching the rain in the palm of her hand.

"That's goin' to ruin the nice squeegee I just gave his windscreen," Tinker said. "Poor guy ended up getting nothing out of meeting us."

"Shame," Chaplin said with a smile. "Some people are just unlucky, I guess."

Tinker laughed and drove on into the rain.

They saw the first sign on the outskirts of Albuquerque: "THE HOLY SPIRIT is COMING! Will you be part of His Grand Crusade?? Miracles! Salvation! Eternal Life! AWAITING YOU! JULY 15-20!" Chaplin sat up straighter and twisted to look at the sign as they passed it. She didn't even have to ask. Tinker was ready when she turned back around to face forward.

"I'll start looking for a room to rent."

"Are you sure?"

Tinker smiled at her. "I don't want you pouting all the way to Arizona."

Chaplin whooped and punched the ceiling of the truck. Tinker couldn't help but laugh at the younger woman's enthusiasm. Church revivals were always a great target, and they hadn't run across one in a few months. They always had plenty of opportunities for fun and profit, more than enough to justify setting down roots for a week or so.

They stopped to get a newspaper to check the listings, then drove through the borderland neighborhoods to take a look at the places being advertised. They didn't stop at any of them, instead making snap judgements based on what they saw driving past. Too exposed, too far from the heart of the city, too close to the heart of the city, too many neighbors. Tinker would eliminate places with a shake of her head. Chaplin knew better than to ask for explanations. She had been doing this long enough that sometimes she didn't even need a reason. If her intuition told her to skip a place, she trusted it and kept driving.

Tinker finally settled on an adobe ranch house a few blocks before the city gave way to desert. The room for rent was a detached building on the back of the property, which was enclosed by a low wall. Tinker looked at Chaplin, who shrugged and nodded. Tinker agreed and parked at the curb. Chaplin remained in the truck while Tinker followed the tile walkway up to the front door.

She knocked, took a step back, squinted to the west as she waited. A few more houses like this one, and then nothing but open desert. The horizon was made up of rocky hills that looked close but she knew from experience were probably a hundred miles away. It was the perfect place to make a quick escape if one became necessary.

She was about to raise her hand to knock again when the door swung open. The woman who answered was younger than expected, but clearly the owner of the house rather than a housekeeper or maid. Her blonde hair was pulled back in a ponytail. Her eyebrows, a shade darker than her hair, were thick and knitted together in an almost angry tangle as she squinted into the sun. She gave Tinker an up-and-down examination, judging her as quickly as Tinker had judged the other places offering rooms, and then craned her neck to look at the truck. Chaplin had the brim of her hat pushed up and her glasses perched low on her nose. Her arm was dangling out the window, and lifted her hand in a lazy wave. The woman didn't wave back, instead refocusing on Tinker.

"You're here about the room?"

"That's right," Tinker said, slightly thrown by the woman's brusqueness. "I'm Edith Byrd and
that's~"

"Don't bother with all that yet," the woman interrupted. She stepped out of the house and closed the door behind her. "Wait until you see the place before we waste time getting to know each other."

Tinker nodded. "That seems like a reasonable course of action."

The woman started out along the side of the house. She motioned for Chaplin to get out of the truck. They followed her to the building on the back of her property, the small stones of the yard rattling under their shoes as they walked. Chaplin jogged to catch up with them, hands in her pockets. The woman looked back at her. She eyed Chaplin's trousers, hat, suspenders, and button-down shirt.

"Are you two roustabouts?"

"No, ma'am," Tinker said.

"She's dressed like one."

Tinker chuckled. "Margie likes to dress comfortable on the road."

The woman didn't respond to that. She unlocked the house and stepped inside, turning on the light as she continued deeper inside.

"Fully furnished, as you can see," she said, her voice echoing. "Utilities are included in the price of rental. You have your own bathroom out here, but laundry room is in the house. Ask before you use it, if you'd be so kind. Just knock on the side door."

Tinker took in the space. Relatively large living room, separate kitchen, a short hallway leading back to what looked like an office, the bathroom, and a bedroom. The woman finished opening windows and came back to join them in the main room. She put her hands on her hips and looked around as if she was the one considering it as a rental.

"It's not much. Only the one bedroom, so one of you will have to be okay with the couch."

"That's fine, fine," Tinker said. "We'll make do. And it's a hundred for the month?"

The woman nodded. "Seeing as it's already the tenth, we can do you a discount for that. Bring you down to sixty."

"Well, that's mighty kind of you, miss," Tinker said. "We'd

sure appreciate that generosity."

Chaplin had spent the conversation meandering along the edge of the room. She peered out the window, squinted at the couch, and tilted her head back to look up at the exposed beams of the ceiling.

"What do you think, Margie?"

Chaplin nodded. "Looks nice."

"I have to agree." Tinker extended her hand to the woman. "I think we have a deal."

The woman came forward and shook her hand. "I suppose now would be the time for names."

"I'm Edith, like I said. Edith Byrd. This is my sister, Margaret."

"Sophia Ellis." She looked at Chaplin, then back at Tinker. "You don't look like sisters."

Tinker laughed. "Dark and fair, what a pair. That's something our daddy used to say."

"Uh huh..."

Tinker knew what was going through the woman's mind. She and Chaplin couldn't have looked more different. Tinker's dark black hair was the complete opposite of Chaplin's lighter auburn braids. But the look on Sophia's face now was probably more about the fact Tinker had a good twenty years on her 'sister.' Tinker didn't say anything. She let the moment hang, putting the decision on Sophia. If she was like most people, she would just let it go.

"Well," Sophia finally said, "I've got some papers in the house. Just to keep everything official and legal-like. I'll go get them, and the two of you can talk. I'll be right back."

"I appreciate it," Tinker said.

Sophia stepped around her and left the house. Tinker waited until she was across the stony yard before she faced Chaplin.

"Well?"

"Looks nice," Chaplin said, nodding slowly. "What do you think, though, draw straws for the bed? Switch off?"

Tinker said, "It's a big bed. We could share it."

Chaplin looked over her shoulder into the bedroom.

"We're both grown-ups," Tinker said, letting some of her exasperation seep into her voice. "It's no big deal. You don't have to take the couch."

"It's fine. The couch looks sturdy and comfortable." Chaplin walked over and tested the cushions. "Besides, if something happened and Sophia happened to see 'sisters' sharing a bed, it might raise a lot of questions."

Tinker sighed and shook her head. "We'll trade off."

"If that's what you think is best."

Tinker looked out the front window to see Sophia was coming back. "We'll work it out later. For now, it's show time, sis."

INTERLUDE

PHILADELPHIA
Saturday September 21, 1940

The first punch was so solid that Chaplin thought the man had to be holding something in his fist. She had braced herself to get hit, prepared to absorb the blow so she could look tough. But to her surprise, the man had really put his full weight into it. He punched her in the side of the head so hard that her ear starting ringing and her knees went out from under her. Luckily his two cohorts tightened their grips on her arms and hauled her back up before she could fall to the ground.

"Lord almighty." She was still seeing stars. "It was dark in there so I didn't know I was playing against Max Baer."

"Hey, she's funny," the puncher said. The cigar in the corner of his mouth bobbed when he spoke. "Maybe you should've stuck to comedy instead of poker."

He punched her again before she could respond. This time his knuckles glanced off her jaw. Her teeth cut her lip, and she spit out blood as she was hauled back to a standing position.

They were in an alley outside a bar called Horseshoe. She'd thought the name would give her luck and, for most of the night, she'd been correct. She'd collected a pretty hefty pot by the time she finally bowed out. Unfortunately Richard, Gabriel, and their punchy friend Lawrence had been waiting outside when she left.

She assured them she hadn't been cheating, even though she had. She wished them better luck at the next game, which they would probably have since they weren't playing against her. But Lawrence had punched her hard in the gut and his friends had dragged her into the alley to finish taking out their anger.

"Look..." She still tasted blood, and her lip was starting to swell. She worked her jaw and looked up at Lawrence. "I get it. No one likes to lose. So let's just call this a friendly game, all right? The dough is in my right pocket. Just take it and we'll go about our nights."

Lawrence cracked his knuckles. "Uh-uh. I don't mind losing in a fair game. But no one's as lucky as you were. You needed an ace? You get an ace. Someone gets a full house? You've got a straight flush. It's downright magical. You magical, Elizabeth?"

Chaplin grinned. "Depends on who you ask."

Lawrence sneered. "All right. Get her hand down."

The men pushed her against the wall. The one holding her right arm brought it up and pinned her wrist against the brick.

"Wait, hold on." Chaplin felt panic starting to creep in. She could take a beating. She didn't mind losing all her profits from the night. "What's going on?"

"We're teaching you your place." Lawrence took a cigar cutter from his coat pocket. "We have an obligation. We can't have you running around stealing money from hard-working men."

Chaplin jerked her arm, but she couldn't get free from the man's grip. "Wait, wait. Hold on."

"Don't worry," Lawrence said, brandishing the cutter. "It's just your pinky finger."

Panic was starting to take over. Chaplin jerked and fought, but the men pinning her to the wall were too strong. Lawrence slipped the ring of the cutter around her pinky.

"Don't~"

"You definitely don't want to do that."

Chaplin and all three men looked toward the new arrival. The alley was too dark, and she was backlit by the streetlamps, but the tip of a cigarette flared as she inhaled.

"Mind your own business, lady," Lawrence said. "She has this coming."

"Oh, I know exactly what she deserves." The woman sauntered

casually into the alley. "I was watching her all night. I was actually trying to figure out how long it would take you fellows to realize she was taking cards out of her sleeve." She laughed. "She wasn't even subtle about it toward the end! So no, I'm not saying stop. Thieves and cheats need to learn their lesson. But... I just want to be sure you're okay with the lesson you're teaching."

Lawrence grunted. "What are you talking about?"

"Her pinky finger...? That's an important digit, friend. It's the anchor of the hand." She held up her own to demonstrated. "It gives you a strong grip. Why, look at your boys holding her to the wall there." Everyone looked at the hands on Chaplin. "See how the pinky is stretched out? She might have a chance of getting away if they didn't have pinkies. You might as well cut off her thumb."

Lawrence wrinkled his lip. He looked down at his hand.

"The forefinger," the woman said. "That's what you want to go with. I know it doesn't seem to make sense, but trust me. Lose that one, you've got a backup right next to it ready to take over. It's the smart choice. And honestly, guys. Losing the pinky would ruin her life. Do you really want to ruin someone's life because of, what was it? Thirty dollars?"

The grip on her wrist became looser.

"Of course she might still bleed out from the wound, no matter which finger you take. So I suppose it's just an academic argument. But on the off chance she does get to a doctor in time..."

"Ah, hell." Lawrence waved his hand. The other two men released Chaplin. "Hand over the cash and we'll call it even."

Chaplin reached into her vest pocket and handed over a few folded bills. "I'll throw in a little extra. The next round is on me. No hard feelings."

Lawrence pocketed it and then looked at the mysterious woman. He hooked a thumb at her. "You're lucky this lady doesn't mind her own business. C'mon, fellas."

They drifted back into the bar. Chaplin waited until they were gone to unlock her knees, putting her hand against the wall to catch herself at the last second before she collapsed. The fear of losing a finger had been very real, and she fought the urge to be sick all over her savior's shoes. She took a few deep breaths before she looked up and eyed the other woman.

"Thanks."

The other woman shrugged. "A woman sees another woman being dragged into an alley by three goons, it's common courtesy to make sure everything is on the up-and-up. Are you okay?"

"I will be. Thanks." She flexed her fingers as if making sure they were all still there. She straightened up and started toward the street. Her face hurt, and her stomach was sore.

"You gotta get better, kid."

Chaplin stopped and looked back. "Better? Are you kidding me? Did you see the size of that wad? I took those guys for everything they had."

"Thirty whole dollars. And look what it nearly cost you."

The other woman caught up with her. She was dressed in a suit and waistcoat, black hair pinned up. She could have been mistaken for a man in the right light, or by someone who's left eye was starting to swell shut. Chaplin guessed the woman had about twenty years on her, but she wore them very well.

"Your problem is that you think getting the win is the finish line. That's like saying you can sail a boat because you know how to get it away from the dock. Winning is the first step. Getting away with the pot, keeping it, that's the skill. Yeah, you were rich tonight. For about five minutes. How much cash you got on you now?"

Chaplin didn't bother checking her pockets.

The woman produced a matchstick from somewhere and bit down on the end. "Being good at the start of the night doesn't mean a damn thing if you suck at the end of it. Remember that before you try this again."

"Sure," Chaplin said as they stepped out onto the sidewalk. "Better. I'll get right on that. I've been out here for ten years. Ten fucking years." She kicked at a piece of trash, sending it ricocheting off the far wall with a clatter. "I manage to get a roof over my head, mostly. Enough to eat most days. Stupid cons like this are the only way I can keep my head above water. All it would take it one bad night and..." She shook her head. "Just one bad night."

"Ten years. Wow. And you've been all by yourself that whole time?"

"I don't need anyone else."

"Yeah, you do." She looked up at the stars, shook her head, then held out her hand. "Tinker."

Chaplin looked at the hand. "What?"

"That's what you can call me. Tinker."

"Just Tinker?"

"For now."

After a minute, Chaplin took the hand. "Penny Chaplin."

"That better not be your real name."

"Of course not," Chaplin said.

Tinker nodded down the street and started walking. "Come on. We can find a diner, talk what we're going to do about your situation. I'll buy you something to eat."

"I don't need your charity."

"You just said a bad night could ruin you, and you lost all your profits."

Chaplin looked at her, confused, and then realized. "Oh, that? No. I gave them fake paper."

"You *what?*"

"I worked hard for that cash! I'm not just going to hand it over because they're scary."

Tinker looked back toward the bar. "You know who is even scarier? The *bartender* who has a *gun* behind his bar. When he finds out that cash is fake, it's not going to take him long to track down where it came from."

Chaplin said, "So..."

"So *run!*"

They ran.

CHAPTER TWO

ALBUQUERQUE
Tuesday July 10, 1945

The couch was *not* fine. Even with her head on the arm, Chaplin's feet had to be propped on the other side. It made her feel like she was in the world's most rigid hammock. She tried the fetal position for a bit, knees drawn up, but the couch was so narrow that she kept almost rolling off when she shifted position. Her evening had been exhausting enough that she still managed to get a few hours of sleep between contorting herself on the cushions.

After bringing in their luggage, such as it was, she took the truck into town for a newspaper. The tent revival was less than a week away, so they still had plenty of time to do some other small jobs while they waited. The paper was a good place to look for potential targets. On the way home she stopped to get some fried chicken for dinner. Tinker had spent the time she was away unpacking.

They separated the paper on the counter separating the living room and the kitchen and skimmed it while they ate dinner. There was potential, there was always potential, and she had a feeling their time in Albuquerque could be very lucrative even before the church people tossed their canvas up.

Chaplin's brain was as much to blame for her restlessness as the couch. She kept going over what they'd read in the newspaper and trying to link stories up with classic con games. It was like she was an actor getting ready to take the stage and she only had half a script. It was exciting, it made her feel alive, but it also made her feel low-level queasy every time.

She finally gave up on sleep at half past four in the morning. She moved silently to get a glass of water, walking on the balls of her feet so she wouldn't wake Tinker.

The window over the sink looked out on the back of the main house. The kitchen light was on and she saw Sophia standing at the stove. She was presumably cooking something, but her hair was a tangled mess and she looked to still be wearing her pajamas.

Chaplin got her glass of water and drank it while she watched the back of Sophia's head. She swayed a little, she moved to the left or right to grab tools or utensils, but otherwise she remained directly in front of the burner with her head slightly bowed forward. By the time Chaplin's glass was empty it had occurred to her that she couldn't see any smoke. Surely if something was being cooked, there'd be some kind of smoke, she thought.

Finally, Sophia stepped away from the stove. She didn't take anything off the burner, but she turned off the light as she left the kitchen. Chaplin looked back toward the stove. No glow of a hot burner. No flickering to indicate a spreading fire.

"Huh..."

She narrowed her eyes and twisted her lips to one side. Part of her thought she should go check it out, just to make sure the woman wasn't about to burn her house down. But there'd been no evidence of anything actually being cooked. The kitchen was pitch-black now. Surely a fire would have made itself known somehow. She drummed her fingers on the counter and finally decided she didn't want to risk being caught breaking into their new landlady's house on their first night in the new place.

She went back to the couch and sat down, draping one leg over the other, resting her head in her hand. She planned to stay there until it was bright enough to read, then she would get out the newspaper and make some solid plans about how they would spend the rest of their week. They couldn't pull anything big, nothing that could blow up in their faces and get them run out of town. A badger game here, a bad Samaritan there. Some of the easiest cons relied on people not knowing she and Tinker were together, so they'd have to make the decision quick before they were seen around town.

As she started to drift off, she thought about how ironic it would be if she managed to fall asleep sitting up. Surely if the couch was too uncomfortable to sleep on lying down, there was no chance she would be able to fall asleep while sitting up...

"You're drooling."

Chaplin jumped. She blinked at the sudden sunlight, twisted away from the suddenly-present and fully-awake Tinker. She stretched, scooted to the front of the couch, and rubbed her hands over her face.

"What time is it?"

"Breakfast time." Tinker opened the icebox and peeked inside. "Eggs and bacon?"

Chaplin grunted an affirmative and grunted as she stood up. "I might change my mind about sharing the bed. That couch belongs in the garbage."

"Rough going?"

"I've had rougher," Chaplin admitted. "But if you're still willing to share..."

Tinker nodded. "Sure." She uncapped the milk and took a cursory sniff that made her head whip back. "Oh, lord. This turned."

"What? That's impossible." Tinker offered her the bottle. She smelled, grunted. "Great. So I guess I'm about to find out what time the grocery store opens."

"Just ask the lady of the house."

Chaplin looked out the front window, thinking about what she'd seen a few hours earlier.

"What's wrong?" Tinker asked.

"Nothing. I just thought we might like to keep things separate."

Tinker shrugged. "It's just milk."

"Yeah, okay. I'll be right back."

She was still in her slacks and a plain white undershirt, and she assumed that was good enough for a brief early morning encounter.

She put on her shoes and headed across the rocky side lawn to knock on the back door. She couldn't see any movement in the kitchen windows but someone called out for her to come in. Chaplin scratched her neck, considered going back to have a dry breakfast, but then let herself inside.

The kitchen had not burned down in the night, and it didn't seem as if it had been put to use yet that day. Chaplin craned her neck to look through the open doorway into the rest of the house. The living room was stuffed full of furniture - a couch that looked infinitely more comfortable than the guest house, armchairs, ottomans - a bookshelf, a desk, three tables that Chaplin could see, and an abundance of lamps.

The thing that drew her attention, however, and tempted her to cross the threshold was the piano tucked against the wall. It had evolved from instrument to desktop, serving as a flat surface to hold stacks of newspapers, magazines, and books. The fallboard was up, which meant the keyboard was dusty, but the keys themselves were intact. She pressed down on one key and it let out a solid, strong note.

It was louder than she expected and it broke her from her trance. She stepped away from the piano and turned around just as Sophia appeared in the doorway.

"Oh," Sophia said. "I thought you were--"

Chaplin's "I'm sorry, I just wanted to--" overlapped with her, and they both fell silent. Chaplin smiled awkwardly and motioned for Sophia to continue.

"I thought you were the milkman." She crossed through the living room and into the kitchen.

Chaplin followed her. "Um, kind of the exact opposite, in fact. The milk I got expired overnight. Edith sent me over to see if you had any to spare."

Sophia laughed. She started taking eggs, bacon, bread, and other breakfast items from various containers around her kitchen.

"I should have an extra bottle when Henry shows up. He knows I like to sleep in, so he's comfortable leaving me 'til last."

"I appreciate it." Chaplin patted her pockets. "I can pay you--"

"Don't even worry about that. Consider it a housewarming gift." She started the toast. "Actually, no. Consider it an apology for how I acted yesterday. I was annoyed and overheated and grumpy. I'm not usually that irritable with people."

Chaplin waved off the apology. "It's fine. I didn't even notice."

"I appreciate it." She rested her hands on her hips and scanned the kitchen for something else to keep herself busy. "You said your milk went bad overnight. Did you get it from Woodman's? The little shop about a mile from here?"

Chaplin tried to remember. "Yeah, I think that was the place."

Sophia shook her head. "That place is a damn joke. I'm sorry I didn't warn you about it. The man who runs it, Clarence? He's never met a penny he can't pinch. He gets away with buying cheap, stocking garbage, because he's the only store in this area. A lot of people have no choice but to shop there because Smith's Market is just too far away. He's just this side of being an all-out thief."

"I'll be sure to avoid him in the future." In reality she was filing away the information to exploit it later. A grocer who pawned off cheap food just to line his own pockets was exactly the kind of mark she and Tinker liked going after. "So, um, I'll get out of your hair. I'll keep an eye out and come back over once the milk has been delivered."

"You don't have to go." Sophia craned her neck to look at the clock hanging over the kitchen door. "He really should be here any minute. No point in having you run back and forth. Unless you have your own breakfast waiting."

Chaplin glanced at the back door. "Uh, no. It can wait, I guess." She was throwing in as many 'uh' and 'hm' pauses as she could. It gave the impression she was thinking slower than she really was, which gave her wiggle room to go through multiple scenarios before she had to make a final decision. "I just don't want to get in your way."

"Oh, you're not bugging me. Honestly, I hate how quiet this place is sometimes. It's nice to have someone around making noise." She pointed to the living room. "The music, in particular. It was really jarring to hear that. In a good way, in a good way. Do you play?"

"I, um." She waved off the question. "I used to."

"Why did you stop?"

"Edith and I move around a lot. A piano isn't exactly something you can just toss in the bed of a pickup truck and take it with you."

Sophia smiled. "That's true. It's kind of a pain. The only reason that one is still here is because it's not worth the trouble getting rid of it."

"Oh, you don't play? I just assumed it was yours."

"No, it was. Is." The tone of Sophia's voice changed. It was softer, but a wall up had gone up. "I don't play it much anymore, either."

"Okay," Chaplin said.

Sophia cleared her throat. "So. So, um, where are you ladies from originally?"

Chaplin's mind clicked to their standard backstory. "Vermont." In their experience, no one knew much of anything about Vermont. "Edith was laid off from her job as a receptionist at the timber mill." Someone in New Mexico wouldn't know anything about that industry. "So we had some savings and decided to see the country while we had a chance."

"That sounds like a lot of fun. Expensive, too."

"We pick up odd jobs to help us pay for what we need."

Sophia started to say something but was interrupted by a knock on the front door. "Ah, there's Henry now. Come on, I'll introduce you."

"Oh I don't..."

But Sophia was already halfway through the living room. Chaplin followed her and hung back as she opened the front door. The man on the porch wore a white shirt and a small black bow tie. He was holding a wire carrier with two glass bottles of milk.

"Morning, Sophia!"

"Good morning, Henry. Listen, would you happen to have an extra bottle on the truck? I have new tenants, and they fell victim to Woodman."

Henry shook his head as he handed Sophia her bottles. "I tell you, the fact that man is still in business is a crime!" He looked past her and saw Chaplin. "Is this your tenant? Morning, miss. Tell you what, I want you to have a good opinion of our town, so I *do* have some extra on the truck and I'll let you have it free of charge."

"Oh. You don't have to do that..."

He was already trotting back to his truck and either didn't hear her or pretended he couldn't. Sophia chuckled and crossed her arms, holding the bottles against her chest with one hand.

"Don't get the wrong impression of our town, Ms. Byrd. We do eventually make people pay for their milk."

"That's good to hear, I guess," Chaplin said.

Henry came back and held out the bottle. "Here you are, miss. One quart, fresh, cold, and pasteurized."

"I really appreciate it."

Sophia said goodbye to Henry and took her milk to the kitchen. Chaplin followed and headed for the back door.

"Thank you again."

"Sure. Just knock if you need anything else. And hey, if you and your sister ever want to join me for dinner, I'd love the company."

Chaplin smiled. "How neighborly. I'll tell Edith about it and we'll let you know."

She left quickly feeling like she had escaped. She'd gotten the feeling Sophia had been holding back on questions she really wanted to ask, like the age difference between her and Tinker. Chaplin had held back as well. There was no way to bring up the early-morning kitchen activity she'd witnessed, at least not casually, or during their first real conversation. She supposed it would have to remain a mystery for the time being.

Tinker was standing at the counter, already eating, when Chaplin came in. "There you are. I was starting to worry you had to find a farm and milk the cow yourself."

"Sorry. I got roped into a conversation with the lady of the house." Tinker already had an empty cup next to her plate. Chaplin opened the bottle and filled the glass. "It wasn't wasted time, though. I found a potential target."

Tinker's eyebrows rose. "Do tell."

"Woodman, the guy who owns the general store." She found that her breakfast was cooked and waiting. She took the plate and sat across from Tinker. "Thanks for this, by the way. Apparently we're not the first customers who have gotten sour milk from him. Cuts corners, raises profits."

"Sounds like potential." Tinker looked past Chaplin, eyes narrowed. "There are a few marketplace cons we could use on him. I'd need to sort it all out a bit more before pulling the trigger. But potential for sure. What about her? The lady? Um, Ellis?"

Chaplin shrugged. "She's a nice lady. No reason to go after her."

"I didn't say anything about going after her," Tinker said. "But point made. The grocer should keep us busy for a day or so anyway."

"Sounds good."

They fell into silence, eating their breakfast. Tinker drank from her glass while Chaplin drank directly from the bottle. She could tell Tinker was mentally planning how she would punish Woodman. Her own mind was preoccupied with the piano. It had been almost fifteen years since she played. She was eighteen. It was New York. And the piano belonged to Addie Pryor...

INTERLUDE

SANDY CREEK, NEW YORK
1930

Adeline Pryor was a very quick learner. Much quicker than they told her parents. In a way, it was Chaplin's first confidence game. Addie was an acquaintance from school. Everyone knew Chaplin could play piano, because she'd been playing at her daddy's church since she was tall enough to sit at the bench. She was a savant, her daddy said, a natural talent. So naturally she was the one that Mr. Pryor sought out when he decided Addie needed to learn an instrument.

So Chaplin, who wasn't called Penny Chaplin at that point, started visiting the Pryor's large mansion on the outskirts of town. The kids called it a mansion because it was larger than any other single residence in Sandy Creek, but there was nothing particularly ornate or wealthy about it. Still, Chaplin had felt awkward and misplaced when the maid let her in for the first lesson.

The piano was in the front room. They were left alone for the lessons, a sliding door blocking most of the noise they produced. They sat next to each other on the bench, Chaplin's right thigh pressing against Addie's left, as she taught her the basics and showed her finger exercises that would make some of the more intricate movements possible.

After just a few weeks, an hour every Tuesday and Thursday afternoon, Addie could keep up with anything Chaplin threw at her. They started playing duets, jazz and ragtime and blues, standards they heard on the radio as well as originals that they made up on the spot. Those were Chaplin's favorites. They never wrote down the songs they made up, and only rarely tried to give them lyrics, but she had rarely been happier than those afternoons when they'd been smashing the keys and laughing out nonsense words that happened to rhyme and match the rhythm.

Addie was the one who suggested lying to her father about her proficiency. She loved the piano. She knew that if her father found out she'd already gotten good, he would force her to move on to some other hobby. To him, the lessons were more about learning a discipline than having fun. Training for training sake, with the skills she attained being little more than side effects.

"He'd put me on a horse next," she said as her fingers danced across the keys. "He'll have the maid waking me at four in the morning just so I can ride a poor animal around in circles for a few hours before class."

So Chaplin accepted payment for lessons she wasn't giving. School ended, they graduated, and the lessons continued. And as they rolled on into the summer, Chaplin started to notice Addie more. The way her fingers moved over the keys, specifically. The way her dresses sometimes fell across her thighs. She had spent so much time watching Addie play that she had almost memorized the pattern of freckles on her wrists and forearms.

"I know the back of your hand like the back of mine," Chaplin said one day.

Addie had laughed. She held up her hands to examine the backs. She reached for Chaplin's wrist and pulled it up until their palms were flat against each other. Addie's skin was soft and warm against Chaplin's. She inhaled but then couldn't seem to breathe out, transfixed by the slight pressure of Addie's hand on hers. Addie's fingers were just a little shorter than Chaplin's. She wanted to lace them together, to squeeze.

"Hm," Addie said. It sounded almost like a laugh. She looked up at Chaplin, and her eyes were very blue. "That's nice."

"It is nice," Chaplin said on the breath she was finally able to release. "I like it."

"You do?"

Chaplin nodded and gave in to temptation. She squeezed Addie's hand.

Kissing seemed like the next logical step. They didn't let go of each other's hands, but Addie's other hand went into Chaplin's hair, pulling her into the kiss. At one point Chaplin gasped to get enough air, thinking that was why she felt lightheaded, but the deep breath didn't help. Addie's bottom lip brushed against hers, and Addie twisted until she was straddling the bench. Chaplin pushed her down and also straddled the bench, then settled on top of her.

Their hands finally came apart to explore. Chaplin was wearing a button-down shirt. Addie did her best to get the shirt open but fumbled with the buttons. Chaplin had an easier job, moving her hand down to the thigh she'd spent so many hours trying not to notice and brushing her palm up over the soft skin. Pushing the dress up. Fingers trembling as she got closer to her hip.

"You can tell me to stop," she said.

"I know," Addie said.

Addie never told her to stop. Chaplin stopped kissing her long enough to sit up and watch Addie's face as she made the next thing happen, the first time she'd ever made it happen for anyone, including herself, and seeing it made the thing happen to her. She pressed herself down against the bench, a poor substitute for what she actually wanted between her legs, and buried her face against Addie's neck to breathe in the perfume she'd been hypnotized by for weeks.

She kissed her way over Addie's jaw, kissed her chin. Addie turned her head and her tongue flickered against the corner of Chaplin's jaw. Addie whispered Chaplin's name, her true name, the name her mother had given her when she was born.

And then there was the heavy scrape of the drawing room door being slid open. "I hope you don't think you can end practice early~"

Chaplin scrambled to get up so fast that she nearly knocked over the bench. Addie flailed her arms a bit to keep from being tumbled to the ground.

Addie's father, Jonah, stood in the doorway like a freed bull. The lower half of his face was concealed by a bushy black beard. His eyes were wide enough to show white all around, which made the dark circle at the center look like burning coals. Addie tugged her dress back into place as she got to her feet, stumbling, leaning against the piano as she tried to turn to face him, tried to get between him and Chaplin, stammering through a thousand words.

"Daddy, wait, no, Daddy, it's... she was..."

He advanced on her. His face was beet red. Chaplin saw what was about to happen. At the same time, as if in a mirror, she saw the rest of Addie's life. Boarding school, most likely. Strictness. Separation from the things she loved, distance from her family, from her home. She was supposed to go to university. She'd fought for most of her teenage years for that opportunity, and Chaplin could see the promise shattering as Jonah Pryce took three long strides across the room and raised his hand to his daughter.

"I forced myself on her," Chaplin said.

Addie and Jonah both looked at her. Jonah swayed. His brow knit in confusion. His hand slowly lowered as if it was becoming heavier with each breath.

"What?" he growled.

"She told me to stop." Chaplin looked at Addie. "I'm sorry, Adeline. I lost control. I-I couldn't help myself. I didn't listen to her. She didn't want me to do it." Her eyes were burning. She didn't know what else to do say, so she just repeated herself. "She told me to stop."

Jonah crossed the room. Addie gasped, "Wait..."

It was the first time anyone had ever hit Chaplin. It knocked her off her feet, but he followed her down and hit her again. She could still hear Addie begging him to stop over the ringing in her ears. She brought her arms up to protect her face so he kicked her once, extremely hard, and she was positive that something inside her broke in half. Breathing suddenly became difficult, like he'd broken some fundamental part of her.

"Get out of here before I kill you," Jonah growled.

Chaplin got up onto her hands and knees. She half-crawled to the door, aware of wetness on her face but with no way of knowing if it was tears or blood.

She ran from the house certain that Jonah was only letting her go so he could retrieve a gun. She ran through the woods so he wouldn't have a clear shot.

She stopped just short of home. She knew that if Jonah hadn't followed her, he would be on the phone to her father explaining what he'd just walked in on. He would use awful, rotten terms to define the situation but it was her fault. It was the narrative she'd given him. Anything that happened as a consequence would be her own doing. But she was okay with that. She could handle the consequences if it meant Addie was safe and protected.

There was nowhere else she could go, so she stayed in the woods. She hunkered down by a tree and sorted through her options as the world got dark around her. She had a little cash on her. Even if she could sneak into her bedroom, there wasn't enough money there to be worth the risk. If her father saw her, she would be trapped. Imprisoned until morning, at the very least. He was probably sorting out his options as well. In his mind, his daughter was not only a deviant but a predator.

It was full night by the time she finally felt safe enough to leave the woods. She walked back toward Addie's house. At the edge of the property she paused to examine the situation. No car parked next to the shed. Maybe they were at her house, waiting for her to show up. Maybe they were driving around Sandy Creek trying to find her.

Either way, she felt it was safe enough to approach. She found Addie's bedroom window and tapped on the glass with her fingernail. When there was no response, she tried again with a knuckle. She kept an eye out all around her to make sure no one was sneaking up. Her heart was pounding loudly enough that it would have covered any footsteps.

She was about to knock again when the curtains fluttered. Addie peered out, gasped, then fumbled with the latch. She pushed up the glass and rested her hands on the sill.

"You have to get out of here. The things they're talking about doing if they catch you..."

"I know." Chaplin put her hand on top of Addie's. "I just had to be sure you were okay. He believed what I said?"

Addie's eyes were shining in the moonlight. "Yes. They're treating me like I got attacked. I want to tell them what really happened—"

"No! Then they'd just turn on both of us. As long as you're safe, I don't care what happens to me."

"Oh." Addie lowered her head and stifled a sob. "You have to know it's not true, though. You know that, right? It's a lie. I wanted you to."

"I know." It still made her heart soar to hear it.

"I wanted it from before the lessons started." She was speaking so quickly that her sentences were blending together. "I-I had already pretty much taught myself to play the piano. Daddy didn't notice, of course. But I thought it would be an excuse to see you a lot. And I hoped that spending a lot of time together would ruin the idea I had of you in my mind. Maybe you would be rude to our maid or to my mother. Or you'd chew with your mouth open. I wanted to find something wrong with you. Would it have been so hard to be terrible in some way?"

Despite everything, Chaplin laughed. "I'm sorry I disappointed you with my perfection."

"It's your one flaw." Addie sniffled and wiped her eye with the hand Chaplin wasn't holding. "I'm sorry."

"You don't have anything to be sorry for. But I have to go."

Addie nodded. "I know."

"No, I have to leave. Sandy Creek, maybe even New York. They think I'm a bad person. A threat. I don't want to know what they'll decide to do with me, so it'll be better if I'm just gone."

Terror passed across Addie's face, but it was quickly overtaken by understanding. "Wait." She left the window and disappeared into the dark of her bedroom. When she came back, she pressed a few folded bills into her hand. "Take this."

"I can't—"

"Shush. It's as much my fault as yours. This is the least I can do. Please be safe."

Chaplin nodded. "I will. I should go before someone comes back."

Addie said, "Thank you. For letting me know you're okay before you disappeared."

"I had to see you one last time."

"I love you."

Chaplin's heart broke. "I love you, too." She leaned in and kissed Addie's lips, crying when she pulled away. "Go. Get back inside before someone comes to check on you."

Addie pulled back and moved the curtain into place. Chaplin waited until the window was secured and the curtain had stopped moving before she walked away. She opened her palm to see how much money she'd been given. Fifteen dollars.

It would be enough. For what, she didn't know, but she knew it would be enough for whatever was ahead of her.

Chapter Three

ALBUQUERQUE
Wednesday July 11, 1945

They spent most of their first full day in Albuquerque preparing to get their revenge on Woodman. It didn't take them long to figure out their angle, but the rest of the afternoon was spent on acquiring props. Chaplin got their typewriter from the truck and composed a letter. While she typed it up, Tinker got to work on making a stack of flyers. It didn't have to be anything fancy or special, just something with enough information to make Woodman sweat. When they finished making their props, they headed out to search the neighborhood. They started at Woodman's and drove in circles until they found a space for sale that would fit their purposes.

The next morning, Tinker woke early and dressed in her best outfit. She added a blond wig and big glasses. She applied makeup in a way that would subtly change the features of her face. Wider mouth with narrower lips, larger eyes, more defined cheekbones. It would disguise her enough that no matter how the con went, she wouldn't be forced to leave town immediately so Woodman didn't recognize her.

When she deemed herself unrecognizable, she took her flyers

and walked the mile to Woodman's grocery store. She found a spot far enough from the front door that she couldn't be accused of blocking traffic, but close enough that the customers (and Woodman) couldn't help but notice her. She held a flyer above her head and raised her voice like a carnival barker.

"The wait is almost over, folks! In just a few short months, you're going to have a choice in your shopping experience!" She handed the first flyer to someone who passed. "Right down the street here, just around the corner, you're going to have the option to patronize a first-class nationwide chain! Good morning, ma'am, please, take a flyer..."

She had only handed out five flyers when Woodman emerged from the store. He watched her for a few seconds before he walked over.

"Excuse me," he said. "Pardon me, ma'am, may I ask what you're doing?"

"Yes, sir, of course you may." She handed him a flyer. "I represent Piggly Wiggly, the first name in self-service grocery stores. We've got a new location coming to Albuquerque this September, and I'm spreading the word."

He skimmed the flyer. "And who might you be?"

"Martha Franjoy, sir, I'm the franchisee who will be managing the store once it's up and running. Pleasure to meet you. Hope you don't mind a little friendly competition, ha-ha!"

Woodman noted the address and twisted to look down the street. "And you intend to open up just around the corner...?"

"Yes sir, yes, that is the plan! All the ducks are in a row. I've got a letter here... just one second."

She reached into her pocket and withdrew an envelope with the Piggly-Wiggly logo emblazoned in the return address space. She handed it over and Woodman took out the letter, skimming the note Chaplin had written explaining that Martha Franjoy was officially approved to open a market proudly bearing the esteemed name Piggly-Wiggly. The bottom of the letter was signed "Clarence Saunders" in big loopy letters.

Very early in her career, Tinker learned that anyone could write a letter to anybody, CEO or businessman or President, and almost always get a letter in return. The letter would come in a branded envelope, on paper with the official letterhead, and whoever it was addressed to would sign their name at the bottom. With a little bit of manipulation, some artwork, and a bit of skill, it was easy enough to end up with a blank piece of paper that would pass as official after a cursory examination.

"We're excited to expand our brand to Albuquerque!" Tinker said, quoting the letter.

Woodman huffed and folded the letter. He pinched his fingers on the fold and slid it to the edge, clearly fighting the urge to rip it in half.

"You'll bleed my business dry!"

"Oh, surely this side of town is large enough to handle us both! You're not afraid of a little friendly competition, are you?"

"I'm... y-you..."

She smiled and batted her eyes at him. "What's the problem, then?"

He shoved the paper back to her. "Put it somewhere else."

"I'm sorry?" Her smile faded.

"There are a lot of other places to put your piggies-whatever. Pick one."

"But I've done my research, sir, and that is a highly trafficked area with plenty of need for another option to—"

He waved his hands. "I don't care. I don't care about any of that. Have you built anything yet? Installed anything?"

"Well, no..."

"Then just put it somewhere else. Somewhere far away from here."

Tinker sighed heavily. "Sir, I have nothing against you or your business. I didn't think it would be such a problem to open another store in this neighborhood. I do not want to start my career as a businesswoman and franchisee with an enemy! So, so, so I think it p-probably would be best if I did open it somewhere else."

Woodman sighed and smiled. "Fantastic!"

"But, no, you see, I *can't*. I paid a deposit. Non-refundable. And if I lose that, I can't afford to buy somewhere else."

"Not my problem." He was already turning away from her.

"Oh, but it is. I'll open in that space just because I have to. But if the deposit wasn't an issue..."

He stopped and glared at her. He had other options, a multitude, and Tinker knew he was flipping through them at that moment. He could let her open the fictional store and make life hell for her until she closed to escape the harassment. He could badmouth her to all of his customers. He could find the real sellers of the storefront and buy it out from under her. He would still lose a small fortune, but it wouldn't benefit her or Chaplin at all.

But it would be so much easier and probably cheaper in the long run to just make the problem go away right now.

"How much is the deposit?" he asked through clenched teeth.

"A thousand."

"A *thousand?*"

She shrugged, as trapped as he was. "That's why it's this or nothing. I can't just lose that much money and start somewhere else."

He worked his jaw, lips twisting. Then he motioned for her to follow him back into the store.

"I'll give you the deposit."

"What?" She trotted to keep up with him. "That's very generous..."

He grunted and shoved the door open. "A bargain compared to having you leech my profits." She followed him through the store, both of them ignoring the curious looks from customers in the aisles. He went into the office, sat behind his desk, and moved his chair to the large safe tucked underneath his bookshelves. "I want you to know this is basically a *gift* to you," he said as he spun the combination. "Running a business like this? It's like setting your money on fire. You think losing a thousand dollars is bad? Hah! That's a strong week for a grocery store! You're going to be so deep in debt that 'broke' is a pleasant memory. An unattainable dream."

Tinker remained silent on the other side of the desk. He counted out five thin stacks of twenties and slammed them down on the desk. When she reached to take it, he put his hand on top of it.

"Other side of town. Better yet, don't open the store at all. Just consider this your escape hatch. Invest in something that actually has promise."

"I'll take that under advisement."

He moved his hand. She took the cash.

"You can't pay off everyone who thinks about buying that shop."

Woodman sighed and slumped back in his chair. "Do you think you're the first person who has tried to muscle in here? Please. You won't be the last, either. It's cheaper to just send you idiots packing." He ran a hand down his face. "I keep waiting for someone to turn it into... I don't know. A yarn shop or something. But no, it's just you lot. I'm almost ready to take the expense and just burn the place down so it will stop haunting me."

Tinker shrugged. "There are plenty of other lots around here. You're bound to have a competitor you can't buy off one of these days. Might be better to give in to the inevitable." She started to leave, slipping the money into her pocket, but she stopped at the door and looked back at him. "Or you could do the smart, economical thing..."

"And what would that be?"

"You could open a yarn shop."

Tinker came into the house and dropped a stack of money on the coffee table. "Your cut."

Chaplin leaned forward and picked it up. "You're kidding. He just handed it over? It's not even lunchtime."

"Apparently we're not the first to think this neighborhood needs competition." She pulled off her wig and glasses, leaving them on the kitchen counter. She wet a washcloth in the sink and scrubbed away the excess makeup, erasing her disguise with a few firm strokes. "He seems to have accepted that this kind of extortion is just the cause of keeping his stranglehold." She went back into the living room, sank into the armchair, and put her feet up on the table.

Chaplin finished counting her money. "Looks like we already justified stopping in Albuquerque. And the revival is still a week away."

"Yep," Tinker agreed. "Not bad for a seat-of-our-pants job. A day of planning, quick execution. If only they could all be like that."

"We got lucky. A bad guy just dropped right into our laps, no snooping required."

"Uh-huh," Tinker said quietly. She put her foot down and leaned forward. "I'm just saying that we could have a lot more days like this... a lot more *paydays* like this... if we were a little less picky."

Chaplin looked at her over the rims of her glasses. "You mean less cautious? Less scrupulous? If we just went after whoever without making sure they deserved it?"

Tinker grunted, wrinkling her nose as if catching a bad scent. She stood up and walked around behind her chair. "I know the rules. Hell, I taught them to you. But we've got to eat, just like everyone else. What do we always say? It's impossible to cheat an honest man. Half our grifts are based on the mark being greedy and trying to get one over on us. I'm not saying we start targeting schoolmarms or little old ladies for their grocery money. All I'm saying is that maybe we're wasting time looking into people beforehand."

"Just because someone falls for a grift doesn't mean they deserve to lose their money."

Tinker sighed and hung her head. "Okay. Let's do a hypothetical. The classic. The violin game. I'm in a restaurant and I can't pay my bill—"

Chaplin rolled her eyes.

"Just follow me, okay? I can't pay my bill. But I have money at my hotel. I just have to run out and get it. So I leave my old beaten-up violin with the restaurant manager as collateral."

"And then I show up and tell the manager that he's holding a priceless Stradivarius. That it could be worth thousands with a little bit of work. Yes, I've played the violin game before a dozen times. With *you*. Jewelry and pocket watches galore."

Tinker came back around the chair. "If the manager is honest, when I come back, he tells me what the 'expert' said. He congratulates me on owning such a wonderful treasure. But if he's greedy... he buys it from me for a pittance. He doesn't care how much it costs, because he'll get his investment back tenfold when he sells the violin."

Chaplin just sighed.

"We don't have to watch the manager. We don't have to know ahead of time what he's going to do when he's faced with the decision."

"What if it's not greed? What if it's desperation? What if his family is struggling—"

"Oh, please. What about the people at the revivals?"

Chaplin said, "That's different. Those people walk into that tent planning to throw money away. All I'm doing is make sure we're in a position to catch a little of it for ourselves. Going after everybody... yeah I suppose it might give us a few extra wins. But there would be just as many losses. It's not worth the time we'd save."

Tinker flipped her hands in the air and dropped back down into the chair. The fight had gone out of her. Chaplin scooted back on the couch, still thumbing through the bills in her hand.

"I taught you too well." Tinker was smiling, but there was some sincere disappointment in her voice. "I created a morality monster."

Chaplin held her hands out palm-up. "It's a defense strategy. If you only go after greedy people, criminals, people who deserve it, there's less chance they'll call the sheriff to go after you. Like Woodman today. Even if he figures out it was a grift, he can't exactly accuse us without admitting to the bribes. Targeting criminals protects us."

"Right, right, right." Tinker pushed herself up out of the chair with a heavy sigh. "It's just that sometimes I think it would be a lot easier if we spent time closer to the edge. I'm going to take a nap. Mind if I take the bed for a few hours?"

"Nope. You did all the hard work on this one, you deserve the mattress."

"Much obliged," Tinker said. "Wake me for dinner."

In the bedroom, with the door closed, she took off her shoes and overshirt and stretched out on top of the blankets still mostly clothed. The night before, she and Chaplin had shared the bed. It was fine. It was hardly the first time they'd slept under the same blankets. She'd still been worried Chaplin would be uncomfortable because of what happened in Oklahoma, or make an issue out of it, but she seemed fine.

Tinker, on the other hand, had spent the night drifting in and out of sleep, careful not to toss and turn. She didn't want to let her guard down and wake up spooning the younger woman. It had happened before, a few times since Oklahoma, and every time resulted in awkward silences and at least half a day of acting inconveniently embarrassed. She hadn't wanted to risk that with Woodman waiting in the morning, so she'd taken the initiative. She stayed up. She made sure she stayed on her side of the bed.

Of course that had the side effect of being aware of Chaplin all night. The sighs she made in her sleep. The snoring. The way the mattress dipped under her weight as she rolled onto her back or repositioned her legs. They were both dressed for bed - Tinker in a shorts and a tank top, Chaplin in one of her gowns - but there hadn't been anything sexual or romantic about it.

At least not where Chaplin was concerned. She'd made that abundantly clear.

It was fine. Tinker took a deep breath and let it out. She folded her hands on top of her stomach and closed her eyes, trying to trick her body into falling asleep.

Chaplin was her partner. Her apprentice. She was young enough to be her daughter, for crying out loud. It was ridiculous to think there was anything more to their partnership than that. Just because they shared the same proclivities, it didn't mean they made sense as anything more than colleagues.

She kept her eyes closed. She told herself if she could fool her brain into falling asleep, she could convince it of anything.

INTERLUDE

NEW ORLEANS

Saturday August 4, 1917

Tinker lay on a bench under the window with an arm draped across her face to block out the sunlight. The arm also served the purpose of hiding her tears. She was twenty-two years old, and as far as she was concerned, her life was over.

"Oh come on now, kid. It can't be all that bad."

"Mind your own business, lady." Tinker lifted her arm and wiped at her eyes. The older woman had already been in the cell when the sheriff threw her in. She was lanky, sitting with big hands resting on spread-wide knees. She wore striped pants covered in patches and a shirt which seemed to have been created by sewing two halves of different shirts together. Tufts of hair stuck out from underneath her straw hat. She did not inspire hope. Tinker had been hoping they could just ignore each other for the duration of their cohabitation. She had far too many things on her mind to worry about conversation.

"Talking always makes it better," the woman said, apparently reading Tinker's mind.

The insistence was enough to make her irritation overpower her fear and sadness. "Talk. You want me to talk? You think it can't be so bad?" She sat up and faced the other woman. "I'm a carny. I've spent the last five years living on a train car with people I would've taken a bullet for. They taught me how to read, how to write, protected me from... from bad people. Last night, a rube goes crying to the sheriff that I'm running a fixed game. Old Hickory rolls up just as we're packing up to go. Slaps a pair of bracelets on me. And these people, my family, the people I've relied on? Suddenly they don't know me. They don't want to get dragged in as accomplices.

"And the really crummy thing about it? I understand why. I probably would have done the same thing if it was someone else. So I'm not even really angry at them for that. But it's the fact that there is absolutely no evidence I was running a crooked game. The booth is packed up and gone. It's my word against the guy's. So when I get in front of the judge, he's going to give me a warning and set me loose. But here's the punchline. It's a circuit court, and the judge won't be here until Monday."

The other woman shrugged. "Seems like you just have to be patient."

Tinker laughed and leaned back. "Oh, it does? Well, then you explain where I'm supposed to go when he sets me free. I have seventy-five cents in my pocket. The carnival is gone, it was rolling out while I was getting arrested. After four days, it's going to be in another state. Everyone I know is on that train, everything I own. My whole life is hundreds of miles away and getting farther with every second, and I don't see a world where I can ever catch up with them."

She dropped her head and caught her breath, rage and fear combating each other in her chest. The other woman was silent for a long time.

"Well. I admit, that does sound like a pretty raw deal, kid. I'm sorry for making light."

Tinker shook her head.

"Okay. Look, it's bleak. I'll admit that. But it's not the end of the world." She got up and moved to sit next to Tinker. She took off her hat, holding it in her hands like a supplicant. "Carnivals survive by advertising. So wherever they end up, they're going to be noisy. All you have to do is keep an ear to the ground and keep your eyes open. You'll track them down eventually. As for funds to catch up with them... well... I may be able to help out there, too."

Tinker looked skeptically at the woman next to her. The

woman's center-parted hair was a wild rat's nest of graying brown tangles.

"You got a few sawbucks hidden away in your sock or something?"

The woman laughed and shook her head. "At the moment? No. That seventy-five cents you mentioned earlier makes you richer than me. But as soon as I'm out of here, I've got some tricks we can use to fill our coffers quick and easy."

"We?" Tinker said. "Our?"

"Sure, kid. I'm not going to give out my trade secrets to some nobody I just met. But some of my tricks need two pairs of hands. You could help me out and I'd cut you in on whatever we take. I can't promise you'll be rolling in gold. But I can keep you fed and sheltered until you get caught up with the carnival. In the meantime, we've got a lot of time to kill in here. I can teach you a few things."

Tinker shook her head. "No offense, lady. But like I said, I spent the last few years with the carnival. Before that, I was raised by people conned, grifted, and stole all day, every day. I doubt there's much you can teach me I don't already know."

The woman chuckled. "First of all, the name isn't 'lady', it's Laffite. And second..."

She held up her hand, revealing three quarters pinched between her thumb and forefinger. Tinker looked at them, unaware of what she was seeing. When she realized, her hand went to her pocket and found it empty.

"What..."

"Your first lesson," Laffite said, holding the coins out. "Never assume you know everything."

Tinker took the coins. She looked at them as if there was some way to prove they were hers, some evidence beyond her own empty pockets.

"Laffite," Tinker said. "Like the pirate."

The other woman shrugged and dipped her head. Not acknowledgement, not denial. Whether the name was from birth or assumed later in life, Tinker couldn't think of a more trustworthy name for a thief in the Big Easy.

"Okay. So assuming you're not magic, how'd you get the coins out of my pocket when I was sitting here staring right at you?"

"Because you *assumed* the coins were in your pocket until I held them up. You just spent the past half hour with your eyes covered, girly. That's a dangerous position when you're dealing with someone who can move without making a sound."

"Move, that's one thing. But you went into my pocket. And I didn't feel anything? That's not possible."

"Stick with me long enough and I won't only prove it, I'll show you how I do it."

Tinker juggled the coins, then folded her fingers around them and chuckled. She put the money back in her pocket.

"Okay, pirate. Show me what you've got."

Chapter Four

ALBUQUERQUE
Wednesday July 11, 1945

Sophia wasn't spying on the new tenants. Well, the only tenants she'd ever had, to be more accurate. But she happened to be washing dishes when the younger one came outside and walked to the truck. Sophia caught the movement in the window above the sink and her eye was naturally drawn to the other woman. She was dressed the same as the last two times Sophia had seen her, slacks and suspenders over a button-down man's shirt open at the collar. Her sleeves were rolled up past the elbows now, and her hair was loose and bouncing with her steps.

Sophia dried her hands and went to the back door. Margaret Byrd had retrieved a box from the back of their truck and was already carrying it back to the guest house. Sophia started to say hello, but her attention was caught by Margaret's bare forearms. The muscles were flexed to hold up the box, which seemed heavy but not unwieldy. She wasn't struggling. But those muscles were working hard. Flexed.

"Is everything okay?" Margaret asked, squinting in the sun.

"Oh. Oh, yes. Sorry. My mind drifted." She waved one hand near her temple like she was clearing an errant thought. "I just wanted to see if tonight was good for dinner. The three of us."

Margaret looked toward the guest house. "Um. I don't think so. Edith had a lot of work to do this morning, and I think she's pretty tired. Definitely sooner and not later, though. We're both looking forward to getting to know you."

"The feeling is mutual!" Sophia smiled and refused to let her eyes drift down to Margaret's arms again. "Well, that looks pretty heavy, so I'll let you go. We'll talk later. Let me know about dinner by five-thirty or so?"

"Will do. Five-thirty. And if your plans change, you know where to find us."

"I surely do," Sophia laughed, waving as she backed up into the house.

She watched through the gauzy curtain until Margaret was out of sight.

"Margaret," she said under her breath. "Maggie? Madge? Peggy? That's a nickname for Margaret right...?" She wrinkled her nose. None of the variations fit the woman, and she certainly didn't seem like a Margaret. She didn't know why she thought that, or what exactly about the woman was un-Margaret. The name just didn't fit the person. Not that Sophia knew her well enough to make such a claim.

She left the window and looked around the house. She tried to see it with new eyes, the way a stranger would. She saw the clutter and dust that she normally overlooked. Maybe it was better if it took Margaret and Edith a while to accept her invitation...

She retrieved the broom and went to work on making the place presentable.

Chaplin emptied the box and lined up forty-eight mason jars on the kitchen counter. Each bell-shaped jar was ten ounces. The silver lids remained in the box for the time being. Once she confirmed the jars were all intact and clean, she began preparing their elixir for the revival show.

It started by making a gallon of sugar water. Two parts sugar to one part water, boiled until the sugar dissolved. Then she added just enough cinnamon extract to give it a little bite. The last step was just a touch of food coloring to give the water a light blue hue. Tinker called it "sapphire sparkle," and it was practically unnoticeable until the jar was held up to the light. It really helped sell their story that the water had mystical properties.

When the main bottle was ready, Chaplin used a funnel to start filling jars. It filled about fourteen of the jars, which she capped and transferred to the icebox to chill until they were ready. Then she started a second gallon. She would need to make four in total to fill all the jars. Not hard work, but tedious and dull. Chaplin still preferred it over making the labels, which made her hand cramp. Tinker was happy enough to do that part and Chaplin was happy to leave it to her.

She looked up when the bedroom door opened. "Hey. Speak of the devil."

"Devil appears." Tinker's eyes were bleary from sleep and her hair was pinned back in wild tangles. She ran her eyes over the remaining jars. "You're making good progress."

"I figured it's better to have the jars ready early just in case another opportunity presents itself. Who knows how many people like Woodman there are in Albuquerque."

"Excellent point." She looked in the box Chaplin had brought in and retrieved the blank stickers and colored markers. "I guess I can get started on the labels."

Chaplin looked at the clock. It was almost five o'clock. "Dang. Before you get busy with that, we got invited to dinner by the lady of the house. She wanted me to let her know our answer by five-thirty."

Tinker spread her art supplies across the dining room table. "Is that a smart idea? We do better when we keep to ourselves. It doesn't really make sense to get cozy with someone we'll probably never see again after next week."

"I'm not suggesting we get cozy," Chaplin said. "But the woman has asked twice. She saw me getting the box and ran out to say hello. She's nosy. If we keep ducking her, it'll only make her pay more attention to us. It would be better to just have dinner with the woman and show her just how boring and mundane we really are. Just two sisters out on a road trip. We might even make her sit through a slide show of photos. We still have those slides we got in Tucson, right?"

"I think so," Tinker said, smiling as she put together Chaplin's plan. "Yeah, I think we've got a few carousels that will dump a bucket of cold water on her curiosity. We just have to be dull for a night. Do you think we can pull it off?"

"Penny Chaplin and Just Tinker? Not a chance." Chaplin smiled and thumped the cap on her latest jar of elixir. "But Margaret and Edith Byrd? Oh yes, those two can definitely put someone to sleep. She'll be sick of those two nudniks by dessert."

Interlude

EASTERN ARKANSAS
Sunday August 8, 1943
"Morning has broken, like the first morning," the congregation sang. "Blackbird has spoken, like the first bird…"

Outside the tent, the day was barreling toward triple-digit temperatures. Half the women in the folding chairs waved fans, while the men had their hats tipped back and angled their faces to catch the breeze. Due to the less-than-Heavenly conditions, the voices of the amateur choir wavered and limped through the verses along with the woman onstage playing the piano.

The loudest voice belonged to a man in a white suit, the Honorable Most Holy Reverend Ephraim "Rumble" Riggs. The Reverend was a beast of a man, six-foot-eight with a barrel of a torso and strangely thin legs. The combination made him look like a bowling ball balanced on two breadsticks. His hair had gone from salt-and-pepper to pure white at some point during the past ten years of revivals.

He held one hand up, partially in praise but mostly to guide their guests through the final chorus. He clutched a Bible to his chest with the other hand, swaying his six-foot-eight body from side to side as if it was the most beautiful song he'd ever heard.

When the hymn ended, he shook his head and held his hand high. "The Lord has sent us angels to serenade us tonight, my goodness! My *goodness*, y'all sound pretty!" He wiped a handkerchief across his sweaty brow as he crossed to his pulpit. "Now that the Lord knows we're all gathered here, I think it's time to let you know what He has to say."

Someone murmured 'amen' just loud enough to be heard.

"Amen!" Riggs bellowed in response, pointing in the general direction of the voice.

"Actually," someone else said, raising her voice to be heard above the reverend. "I think most of these folks would like to just get back inside with their ceiling fans or fancy new air conditioning." She was standing now, a woman in a boater hat and a green button-down shirt and white trousers held up by thick suspenders. She kept her left hand behind her back as she stepped into the aisle. "We may have been singing praises to Heaven, but it feels more like the Devil's domain in here, don't you fine folks think?"

There was scattered laughter, a few people looking around as if uncertain whether this was part of the show or not. Riggs chuckled and strived to keep his mood elevated.

"Ma'am, I appreciate your enthusiasm, but I think everyone would be grateful if you'd allow me to continue with~"

"You can continue." She held up her hand to stop him speaking even as she was interrupting. "And please, don't call me ma'am. My name is Byrd, Margaret Byrd, and I'm sure a lot of these people plan to stick around for the whole thing. But phew..." She pinched her collar and used it to fan herself. "At least a few of them are here for one thing and one thing only. And that's healing, Reverend Riggs. Divine healing that flows through your hands. Is that right?"

Riggs chuckled. He glanced at June, his piano player, who gave him the slightest of shrugs. Then he looked past her to Osker, who looked ready to move in at the slightest hint of permission. Riggs looked at the interloper again.

"If the Lord sees fit, my dear, only if the Lord sees fit."

"Now see... that's where I have a problem." She walked forward, closer to the stage. "These people sit out here in this unholy heat for hours on end, they pay their tithe to the church, sing their songs, and then they don't even get a guarantee that they'll be healed of what ails them." She put a hand on a woman's shoulder and met her eyes. They shared a sympathetic look. "It doesn't seem fair."

"The Lord never gives us more than we can handle."

"That's true, that is true." She was right in front of the stage now. "But He also tells us there's more than one road to salvation."

She turned to face the crowd and held her right arm out, her left still hidden behind her back. Riggs looked at the hand she'd been concealing since she started talking, but the tail of her shirt was draped over it in a way that had to be deliberate.

"Who is here for the healing touch of Reverend Rumble Riggs?" A few dozen hands went up. Margaret whistled. "That's a lot of people. Even if you heal one person per minute, that's a whole extra half hour, forty-five minutes spent in this oven. Surely God doesn't want his people to suffer when they've already suffered so very much."

Riggs reached down but stopped just short of touching her. "Ma'am. Miss Byrd. I think you need to..."

She stepped out of his reach. "I am offering to take some of the load from your admittedly wide shoulders, Reverend. Now, I don't claim to share your healing touch. But I have been blessed with something just as good. Oh, yes, the Lord has seen fit to grant me a elixir of revitalization."

Margaret took her hand from behind her back, holding a mason jar out in front of her as if she had just unearthed a diamond. The liquid inside looked unnaturally blue when the light hit it.

"This miracle water bubbles up from a spring on the property my sister and I own. Our mother had terrible arthritis before she drank her first sip and the next day?" She snapped her fingers. "Gone! Like it never existed. Every sickness, every ailment a Byrd has ever had, it never takes more than one bottle to bring us back to normal and put us right back to doing the work that needs to be done.

"Now, Reverend, I would never dream of trying to steal your followers from you. But the Lord works in mysterious ways, as you yourself has said. I believe he put me here, with bottles of our elixir, to spare the most desperate among your flock from unnecessary suffering. I am making this offer to those who can't bear to spend another minute in this heat, who know that hearing a sermon - no matter how enriching to the soul it may be - will only compound your agony."

People were shifting in their folding chairs now.

Riggs cleared his throat. "N-now, ladies and gentlemen, we-we don't... the message leads to the healing. The praise leads to the healing. Opening your hearts, minds, *spirits* to the Lord is what makes the healing work..."

"Maybe that's why I can't use my hands," Margaret Byrd said. "But I have been granted the gift to help in my own way."

"You cannot hope to enter Heaven by taking shortcuts and backroads!"

Margaret said, "Pray for salvation, but swim for shore! I am giving you the ability to swim, ladies and gentlemen." She pointed to the open flaps of the tent. "Right through there, you'll find my sister. Two dollars, just two dollars for the only jar of elixir you'll ever need. And then you can be on your way without sweating your souls out in this tent."

People rose from their seats and moved for the exit.

"Wait!" Riggs jumped off the stage and stepped in front of Margaret. He watched as the entire congregation filed out of the tent, leaving every chair empty. He was almost a full foot taller than her, and twice as wide. He expected to see terror when he spun to face her. Instead, her head was tilted back and she smiled up at him. "What the hell do you think you're doing?"

"I'm doing the same thing you are." Margaret broke the seal on the mason jar's lid and unscrewed it. "I'm just doing it much faster and saving everyone some time." She held the jar out to him. "Care for a drink? You're positively dripping sweat."

He swatted her hand. The jar shattered on the ground, but neither of them looked toward it.

"I'll wring your neck."

She lifted her chin, exposing her throat. "This neck? This very pale neck that surely bruises very easily and very quickly? What do you think those fine people will think if I walk out of here with fingerprints on my throat? Or a black eye? The only possible culprits would be you or that man trying to sneak up behind me."

Riggs looked at Osker, who stuttered a step when he realized he had been caught.

Margaret Byrd smiled at him. "Sorry you wasted such a hot afternoon, Rumble. Win some, lose some. Maybe you can stick around an extra day. Whole new crowd tomorrow."

"I suggest you watch your back, Miss Byrd."

She shrugged and stepped around him. "I will. Hopefully we

won't end up in the same town again, Rumble. But if we do... you might want to think about skipping the hymns and getting right to taking tithe. Just to get it out of the way."

She laughed as she walked out of the tent, waving goodbye over her shoulder.

Riggs narrowed his eyes and breathed until the burning feeling left his face. There was nothing they could do now, not with a whole slew of witnesses who could blab to the police if he tried to strongarm these girls out of his way. Osker stepped up next to him.

"Watch her. And her sister. Find out *everything*."

"What do you want me to do with what I find?" Osker asked.

"We'll figure that out. In due time."

CHAPTER FIVE

ALBUQUERQUE
Wednesday July 11, 1945

Chaplin went over to tell Sophia they would definitely be there for dinner. When she offered to help, Sophia held up her hands to block her from coming inside. "Just bring yourselves. Seven o'clock?" Chaplin agreed and went back to the guest house to get ready. The first thing she did was go through her bag for anything that would be appropriate for having dinner at someone's house. She didn't think Sophia was expecting anything fancy, but she also didn't want to show up in something threadbare, unwashed, or sun-faded. Too many of her things were at least two out of three.

"What are you looking for?" Tinker asked, coming into the bedroom.

"Something presentable. Where's the banker suit?"

Tinker nodded toward the closet. "I brought it in with the other costumes. Banker suit should be on top." She sipped her water as Chaplin retrieved the bag of outfits they wore for their jobs. "Is there a dress code for this thing?"

"No. I just want to look sort of nice, you know?" She pulled out a dress shirt and gave it a sniff test. She couldn't remember the last time she had worn it, let alone washed it. It was wrinkled, but she could hang it in the bathroom while she showered. That would be as good as pressing it, right? She held it up to Tinker for her approval. "What do you think?"

"Yeah. You look good in that." Tinker looked down at herself. She was still wearing the clothes of aspiring small business owner Martha Franjoy. "Will this be okay?"

Chaplin scanned her. "Yeah, that should be fine." She found a pair of slacks that matched the shirt. She draped them both over her arm. "I'm going to take a shower. We're supposed to be over there at seven, which gives you time to shower before we leave."

"Shower?" Tinker followed her but stopped at the bathroom door. "What's going on? I thought you just wanted to bore her into ignoring us. Is this lady a target?"

"No! Of course not. No." She shook her head.

Tinker smiled as realization dawned. "You want to make a good impression."

It was at times like this that Chaplin hated being so fair-skinned. It was ridiculously easy to tell when she was blushing.

"Aw, you're cute." Tinker chucked under her breath and backed away from the bathroom. "I'll do my best not to embarrass you."

Chaplin pressed her lips together and shut the bathroom door.

In the shower, she rested her head against the tile and let the water wash down her back. Now that she was alone, she had to admit that she might in fact be attracted to Sophia. She was beautiful, and it had been a while since she had any dalliances. But it still felt awkward talking openly about it with Tinker. Since Oklahoma... and their 'Conversation'... Tinker claimed everything was fine. But if you have to tell the other person that things are fine, then things obviously *aren't* fine, and Chaplin wasn't sure which one of them was supposed to do the work to make it better.

The house was hot enough that her hair had already started to dry by the time she finished dressing after the shower. She went back into the living room to find Tinker applying a label to one of the bottles. Chaplin picked up one that was finished and read the label.

"Byrd Sisters Miraculous Spring Elixir." There was a drawing of a small natural spring between two rocks. Tinker drew every label by hand, a touch that took ages but really helped sell the fact it was just two sisters trying to make a few bucks. "You're getting better at the artwork."

"Thanks. I think it's best~"

Tinker glanced up but quickly looked back down at her work. Chaplin looked down to see what had caused the distraction and realized she hadn't finished buttoning her shirt. The lace of her brassiere was visible. She turned to the side and did up the last few buttons.

"I think it's best if I don't get too good," Tinker continued as if the interruption hadn't happened. "We want to look like amateurs. Anything too practiced or professional is going to raise eyebrows."

Chaplin nodded her agreement. She started transferring the labeled jars to the icebox.

"Is there a plan on what we're going to tell the lady?"

"Who?" Chaplin asked. "Sophia? Why does she have to know anything?"

"Because she's going to ask why we're in town, how we make money, what our plans are. You did expect to make conversation during this dinner party right? That's what normal people do."

Chaplin was surprised at herself for not thinking ahead. "You have a point. I don't know why I didn't think of that."

Tinker said, "You're not used to talking to people outside the frame of a job. But we still have to talk to the woman. This time the con is making her believe we're just boring, dull drifters, like you said. That's the goal. So come on, let's hash it out so we're not riffing over the mashed potatoes. She already knows we're sisters on a road trip. What's the next piece?"

"Our money comes from a trust our parents set up for us. We decided to use it to see the country. From here we're going to the Grand Canyon, Los Angeles, then up to the Pacific Northwest."

"Where are we from?" Tinker asked.

Chaplin said, "New York. Keep it simple. Neither of us has an accent that will make her question that, and I can cover any follow-ups she might have."

Tinker shrugged. "Works for me. Are we married?"

"Widowed. You, you're widowed."

"Why me?"

Chaplin raised her eyebrows.

Tinker rolled her eyes. "Fine, the old woman is the widow."

Chaplin snickered. "Not old, just older."

"Sure, sure." Tinker smiled and winked at her, then looked at the clock. "I guess I should get ready, too. I'll finish up the labels tomorrow."

"Works for me. I like the new design."

"Thanks."

Tinker went into the bathroom and shut the door behind her.

Chaplin went to the front window and stood to one side of it. She peeked between the wall and the curtain, not moving it so she wouldn't draw attention to her spying. It was harder to see into the kitchen of the main house in daylight, obviously, but she could still make out the shape of Sophia moving around behind the glass.

She wasn't concerned about the story she and Tinker would tell. They had made up convincing biographies all the way down the Appalachians, across the Gulf coast, without a hiccup. After five years they were good enough at reading each other's minds that she didn't think they'd get tripped up.

But she was intrigued by Sophia Ellis' story. Much more intrigued than she should be, given the woman was just a means to an end. She wasn't a mark. So it didn't matter what her opinion of them was. But Chaplin still cared. And she was very curious to see what she could learn about Sophia's late-night trip to the kitchen.

She leaned her shoulder against the wall and looked at the closed bathroom door. Oklahoma hadn't been that long ago. Just a few months, another bathroom, five hundred miles away from this one. It might as well have been on a distant planet given how different that night had been. Below-freezing temperatures and snow on the ground...

Chaplin listened to the sound of falling water and let her mind wander back...

INTERLUDE

OKLAHOMA CITY, OKLAHOMA
Sunday Christmas Eve, 1944

Chaplin counted it four times before she allowed herself to believe the final tally. Three thousand four hundred dollars. Tinker's eyes had widened when she saw the figure. She had insisted on counting it herself. Chaplin wasn't offended. She was grateful to have the verification. When the last bill was put away, Tinker confirmed the total with a whoop and a cheer.

They were sitting in their truck, the windshield obscured by a blanket of impossibly fluffy snowflakes. The money was in a leather satchel on the seat between them. It was supposed to have been a normal bait-and-switch scam. Chaplin, young and attractive and distraught, would approach a shopkeeper and claim she'd lost her engagement ring somewhere in his store. It was an heirloom, a real diamond, a priceless gem, whatever lie she had to tell. She didn't have time to stay and look, because her fiancé would be home soon and expected dinner. She would leave an address and a telephone number in case he found it. She would promise him a large reward, in this case, three thousand dollars. When she reported back to Tinker, she claimed she had seen dollar signs appear in his eyes.

Fifteen minutes to an hour after Chaplin left, Tinker entered.

Down on her luck, maybe some gray streaks added to her hair, old and much-patched clothes. The shop owner had been on his hands and knees looking under shelves for the ring, but Tinker would be the lucky one. She would find the ring. When the scam went well, the shop owner's greed would overtake him. He would offer to buy the ring from her for what seemed like an outrageous price. Maybe two hundred dollars if they were lucky, five if they were blessed. Poor Woman Tinker would take the money, and the shop owner would try to get in touch with Chaplin to receive his reward. He would find the number disconnected, and Tinker and Chaplin would hopefully be in the next town by the time he accepted he'd been conned.

Everything had gone perfectly according to plan for Chaplin's part. But Tinker made a mistake by arriving too early. There was another customer who had overheard the conversation between Chaplin and the shop owner. He believed he knew the value of the ring, and he'd overheard Chaplin's contact details. So when Tinker 'found' the ring, and the shop owner offered to buy it off her, the other customer stepped in with his own bid.

Tinker had rolled with the improvisation, acting overwhelmed as the men raised the price for each other. By the time she walked out, a stunned Tinker had nineteen hundred dollars in her purse. The other customer had left when Tinker took the shop owner's bid, claiming it was too rich for his blood. Tinker had given the ring to the shop owner, taken the money, and hurried back to where Chaplin was waiting.

"Give me another ring."

"What? Did something go~"

"Hurry!"

They had a whole box full of identical rings. Chaplin plucked one out and handed it over, and Tinker ran back the way she'd come. She caught up with the other customer.

"I'm so glad I caught you!" she said. "I didn't trust that man. He seemed very suspicious. But you seem like an honest man. So if... if you promise you'll get the ring to the proper owner, I'll sell it to you."

He swore on his life that the ring would get a good home. Tinker was so relieved that she was willing to take one of his lower offers... fifteen hundred dollars. There were actual tears in Tinker's eyes when he handed her the bills. She didn't know why he had so much cash on his person, but he looked like it was a pittance to him. His shoes were finely polished. His suit was tailored. Next to him, in her Poor Woman outfit, Tinker felt like a doll that had been dragged behind a truck.

A doll that now had three thousand dollars folded in her purse in exchange for a pair of rings that had cost them two bucks at a garage sale.

It was their biggest haul to date. It was almost too much money. Tinker's mind couldn't even comprehend the fact they could do literally anything they wanted. They could buy a brand-new truck, fresh off the lot. They could buy train tickets to Los Angeles and then another one to New York. The entire country was theirs for the taking.

What happened next was entirely due to emotions with no rational thought behind it whatsoever. Chaplin was so energized and excited at the world of possibilities before them that she leaned across the seat, grabbed Tinker's face with both hands, and pulled her in for a kiss. In her mind, the part that was still connected to reality and consequences, the kiss was a simple elevation from a firm handshake. They couldn't have hugged in the confines of the truck, so this was the next best thing.

But then Tinker changed the angle of her head. Her bottom lip caught on Chaplin's top lip, and then their mouths were open and they were still kissing. And then tongue, and then the brush of her pants across the fabric of the seat. She still didn't know if she moved or if Tinker had pulled her. Tinker's hands had been on her at the time, right above her belt, but Chaplin knew she was responsible for at least half of the change in position.

Whoever was responsible for the move, Tinker was definitely the one who stopped Chaplin from climbing onto her lap. She was the one who stopped the kiss and looked away with a shake of her head.

"What's wrong?" Chaplin asked. She brushed two fingers across Tinker's lips.

"This ain't..." Tinker chewed her bottom lip and stared ahead as if she could see through the snow to the road. "We should get going before someone gets wise."

Chaplin returned to her side of the truck. "Everything okay?"

Tinker smiled tightly at her and nodded. "Everything's fine. It was a lovely kiss. It was very... lovely." She tucked her hair behind her ears and started the engine. The windshield wipers shooped through the accumulated snow. "But we should leave it at that."

Chaplin wanted to argue, but it was clear Tinker was in no mood for it. So she pulled the bag of cash onto her lap and accepted that whatever moment they'd fallen into had passed.

They were staying at a motel in a small town twenty miles outside of Oklahoma City. Neither of them spoke for the duration of the trip, though the kiss hung between them like it was a hitchhiker they'd picked up before leaving town. Tinker parked a few doors down from their room, a standard practice that usually gave them a few minutes if one of their marks came looking for them, and Chaplin tucked the bag under her arm.

Their room was absolutely freezing, and so far during their stay the radiator had proven less than reliable. Tinker shook the snow from her hair, which seemed to be a tactic to keep herself from meeting Chaplin's gaze.

"I'm going to take a bath."

She was in the bathroom with the door closed before Chaplin could reply.

Chaplin paced toward the bed, back to the window, then looked at the bathroom again. She heard the water running, the tub filling. She knew exactly what Tinker wanted to happen back in the truck. The woman wasn't exactly subtle about her attraction, but before now she hadn't done anything about it. But Chaplin knew the only reason nothing had happened between them was because of her. She liked Tinker just fine as a friend, partner, colleague. She loved her, in her own way. It wasn't a romantic love, and she didn't want to risk everything they had for something purely physical.

At least not until right now, tonight, when her entire body was buzzing in search of release.

She steeled herself and went to the bathroom door. She knocked, then let herself in.

Tinker was settled in the bathtub. She sat up straighter and put a hand across her chest. "Chaplin? What's going on?"

"It's after midnight." Chaplin bent down and brought her foot up so she could untie her shoe without sitting down. "I decided I wanted to give you your Christmas present."

"What are you talking about?"

She dropped her shoes and straightened up, unfastening her belt. "It's actually something we both want."

Tinker pressed her lips together, her eyes going cold. "Chaplin. *Penny.* No. I know... I know you don't want this."

"You're a beautiful woman," Chaplin dropped her pants and

stepped out of them to approach the tub. "You want me, right?"

"I-I... I think this is an emotional... night... and you're not thinking clearly..."

Chaplin unbuttoned her shirt but left it on, standing next to the tub in her underwear. Tinker was shifting her legs under the water, hips twisted, and she still had her arm across her breasts.

"Look," Chaplin said, "we can forget this happened. Everything, even the kiss. But are you honestly telling me you don't want this? I know how you feel about me, Tinker. And even though I don't feel the same way, I *do* love you. And right now, I want this to happen."

"And what about tomorrow?" Tinker's voice was sharp. She was suddenly angry. "When you regret it? Or when I think I've finally gotten what I want, then realize you're not offering it anymore? I want more than one night, Penny. And having it once just to know exactly what I'm missing sounds like absolute torture."

Chaplin crouched down and rested her arms on the edge of the tub. "What do you think you'll regret more? When we get to the end of the road, whatever that looks like, which memory would make you happier? Knowing you made the smart decision right here, right now, when everything you wanted was being offered to you? Or knowing that even if you couldn't have everything you wanted, you still got to have one special night with someone who cared very much for you?"

Tinker closed her eyes. "I love you, Penny."

"I love you, too."

"Not in the same way."

"Does that matter right now? Honestly?"

Tinker leaned closer and put her head down on Chaplin's crossed arms. Chaplin kissed her hair. After a minute or two, Tinker sat up and pressed her lips to Chaplin's. This time it took longer for the kiss to become passionate. Chaplin wasn't willing to cross the line and Tinker was still wary of taking everything she wanted. Chaplin could feel Tinker's lips trembling against hers and didn't want to do anything to scare her away.

"It's okay," Chaplin said when Tinker pulled away.

"Are you absolutely sure?" Tinker asked. "You need to be positive you won't regret it. I might be able to take anything else, but if you regretted—"

Chaplin stood up and stepped over the edge of the tub. She was careful not to slip as she straddled Tinker's legs and lowered herself down. The water rose around them, getting perilously close to the edge but not cresting just yet. Chaplin still had on her shirt and underwear but she didn't care. She looked down into Tinker's eyes and saw things she'd never seen there before. Worry, uncertainty, fear.

She cupped Tinker's face in both hands and leaned in to kiss her again. After a moment, Tinker's arms went around her waist and pulled her closer. Chaplin moaned and nodded, moving her hands to the back of Tinker's head as she rocked forward, pressing against Tinker's stomach. She pulled back and whispered Tinker's name. Tinker opened her eyes.

"This is just for tonight, Tinker. But it's all night. Until morning."

"I understand."

"I'm going to give you everything you want." Chaplin spread her fingers on the nape of Tinker's neck. She applied pressure, which made Tinker's eyes roll back. "But you have to let me know what you want. You have to tell me. Or show me. Or just take it. Okay?"

"Okay," Tinker said softly.

Then they were kissing again. Water splashed over the edge of the tub and, before they finally moved to the bed, they had risked causing serious water damage to the tile floor.

Eventually, lying next to each other in bed, Chaplin looked over at Tinker. Her face was sweaty, her lips were wet, and she was staring at the ceiling like her brain had popped. Chaplin reached out and brushed the back of her hand over Tinker's hip. The contact startled her, made her blink, and she turned her head to meet Chaplin's eyes.

"Everything okay?"

Tinker blinked again. Nodded. Then she looked at the ceiling again. "Just for tonight." Her eyes moved toward the window, which was dim with dawn. "Just for this morning. Christmas magic, right? Now we go back to just... what we were."

"Right." Chaplin heard the uncertainty in her own voice. It had been her idea, but after the night they'd just shared, she wasn't so sure it was the right choice. "If we need to have a more thorough conversation about it—"

"We just did," Tinker interrupted. "This was the Conversation."

Chaplin could hear the capitalization in the word. She nodded and looked at the ceiling.

They laid together on top of the blankets, richer than they had ever been, sated if not satisfied, and listened to the snow and sleet rattle against the motel room windows.

A few hours later, when the radio said the roads were passable, they dressed and packed up to head out for their next stop. They weren't sure where they were going, they never knew, but Tinker had a few candidates picked out. Their time on the road would be spent locking in on a target. Chaplin caught Tinker's eye a few times, but she could tell that they weren't going to talk about what had happened the night before. Not now, not ever. The Conversation was all that needed to be said.

In the parking lot, Chaplin swept the snow from their windows and kicked away the dunes that had accumulated behind the tires. Tinker checked to make sure they still had their treasure trove safely tucked away.

"Do you want to drive?" Chaplin asked.

"You can take the first leg."

Chaplin nodded.

When they crossed the town limits, Chaplin looked over. "Merry Christmas, by the way."

Tinker smiled. "Merry Christmas, Chaplin. Thank you."

Chaplin breathed in, let it out slowly. And that, she knew, was the end of the Conversation.

What else needed to be said?

Chapter Six

ALBUQUERQUE
Wednesday July 11, 1945

The kitchen windows of the main house shined invitingly, a golden glow that spilled across the gravel. Chaplin wasn't sure if they should knock on the kitchen door or go around to the front, like real guests. Fortunately Sophia saw them coming and opened the kitchen door before they had to make a decision. She was wearing a sleeveless white shirt with a red neckerchief tucked into the collar like an ascot. Her hair was pushed back away from her face with a red hairband.

"Welcome, welcome." She ushered them inside. "Your timing is perfect. It's almost ready, just a few more finishing touches. Can I get you something to drink?"

"I'm fine," Tinker said.

Chaplin shook her head. "I can help out in the kitchen if you need a hand."

"That would be great. Edith, just make yourself comfortable."

"Will do."

Tinker wandered through the open door to the living room. She saw the piano Chaplin had mentioned, but the room was far less cluttered than reported. It made sense that Sophia had probably cleaned up in anticipation of guests. She wandered toward the bookshelf and tilted her head to the side so she could read the spines. Novels, mostly, which she could appreciate. She didn't mind non-fiction, even though those books reminded her of school.

She could hear Chaplin talking to Sophia in the kitchen, but not what they were saying. She was about to go join them when something shiny caught her eye.

A pocket watch was sitting on the bookshelf, left there almost carelessly. Its chain was curled and jumbled underneath it like a pillow for the actual watch to rest upon. Tinker moved closer and leaned in. She kept her face neutral but her heart pounded as she took in the fine engraving, tuned out the voices to see if she could hear it ticking.

"...dith? Is everything okay?"

She turned to see Chaplin and Sophia in the kitchen doorway. Sophia was the one who'd spoken, raising her eyebrows as she waited for Tinker to answer her.

"I, uh. I'm sorry. I was reading the spines."

"I recognize the sideways head-turn," Sophia said, chuckling. "I was just apologizing for how rude I was to you and your sister yesterday."

Tinker said, "Ironic that I missed it because I was being rude to you."

"I think we can call it even, then. Dinner is ready."

"Fantastic."

She caught Chaplin's eye as she passed. Chaplin knew Tinker had seen something that piqued her interest, but both knew it would have to wait until they were alone to be discussed.

The dinner table was a four-top. Tinker and Chaplin sat facing each other, and Sophia took the chair with her back to the living room. Tinker could see the bookshelf over Sophia's shoulder and it kept drawing her eye, as if there was a sunbeam shining down onto the pocket watch.

Sophia had made something called carne adovada, which almost smelled good enough to distract Tinker from her thoughts. She didn't want to make Sophia suspicious, so she took one of the tortillas and focused on enjoying the meal. She sequestered the part of her brain obsessing over the watch and forced herself to pay attention to what Chaplin and Sophia were saying.

"...moved in here after my parents died. At first I was just going to straighten things up, look for a buyer, that sort of thing, but eventually it was just easier to settle in and take over myself." Sophia paused to take a bite. She swallowed, licked some sauce from her lips. "The house is more than big enough for me, so the guest house was just going to waste. I figured why not make it something useful and help pay for the repairs this place needed?"

"Seems smart to me," Tinker said. "This is really delicious, by the way."

Sophia smiled proudly. "Thank you! It's one of the first meals I learned how to cook, so I tend to overuse it."

"We may have to come over for dinner more often," Chaplin said.

Sophia laughed, and Tinker looked at Chaplin trying to see if she was being sincere or just playing a role. To her surprise, it was hard to tell.

They filled the evening with idle chat about the Byrd sisters. They took turns listing places they'd been, where they hoped to go next, people they had met. The details were familiar and comfortable. It felt like reciting the plot of a book they had read a long time ago. She did her best to keep up a polite conversation, but anything Sophia said went in one ear and out the other. Chaplin was used to picking up the slack when Tinker dropped it, so she carried on without hesitation or slipping up. Sophia laughed at the appropriate spots, asked good follow-up questions, and soon Tinker was surprised to find her plate was empty.

"Would you like dessert?" Sophia stood and reached for their dishes.

Tinker stopped her. "You can get dessert, but I'll take care of these. I insist."

"Thank you very much. I ran out to the store earlier and got some wonderful cupcakes. I did *not* go to Woodman's, thank you very much. Have you ladies been able to get out and find the alternatives? I know you went out somewhere this morning, Edith."

Tinker perked up, turning away from the sink. "You do?" If she'd seen her in costume...

"Well, your truck was gone. I assumed you were looking for the other stores."

"Oh. Right, yes. I was mainly trying to get a general idea of the city. Do you have any suggestions for places that are more trustworthy?"

Sophia held up the cupcakes as she carried them to the table. "I got these from Smith's. It's a bit of a drive, but worth it for groceries you can rely on. And much better than driving back to Woodman's and trying to get a refund for anything."

"I'll make a note. You two go ahead and have yours. I'll finish the dishes and take mine to go."

Sophia sat down again and presented one of the cupcakes to Chaplin. Tinker ran the water as they continued talking. As she washed away the smeared sauce, her brain poked her about the watch again. Could she ask about it? No. Drawing attention to it would be the worst thing she could do. If she brought it up and then it suddenly went missing, they would be the prime suspects. But she had to get a closer look. She had to know if it was worth the trouble her mind was trying to get her into.

She finished the dishes and went to the living room. Sophia and Chaplin were sitting on the couch, angled to face each other, talking quietly. For some reason the sight of it, the intimacy of it, raised Tinker's ire. Even though she'd volunteered to do the dishes, suddenly she felt like she was the help, banished to the kitchen like a non-entity.

She pushed down her irritation and cleared her throat to get Chaplin's attention. "We should probably get out of Sophia's hair."

"Oh, are you sure?" Sophia looked at the clock. "Goodness, I suppose it is pretty late. But we have to do it again soon. It's so wonderful having company, and having someone to cook for."

Chaplin nodded. "Absolutely. We'll figure out a day that works for everyone."

They said their goodnights and left Sophia to finish cleaning up.

Chaplin waited until they were inside with the door closed before she spoke up. "Okay, what the hell was that? You were completely shut-down in there."

"It doesn't look like she cared very much. She only had eyes and ears for one of us. She probably wouldn't have heard a word I said, even if I had tried to say something."

"You're crazy," Chaplin said, but she ducked her head and tucked her hair behind her ears. She was acting like a teenager with a crush, and Tinker's anger threatened to rise again.

"Was she suspicious?" Tinker asked.

"No, she didn't even notice." Chaplin opened the door to the guest house. "What's going on? You were acting weird as soon as we walked in."

Tinker shook her head. "Not as soon as we walked in. After I got a chance to look around." She moved closer to Chaplin and lowered her voice. Even though they were in the relative privacy of the guest house now, she didn't want to take any chances. "She has a pocket watch on her bookshelf."

"So?"

"A *gold* pocket watch. And it's old, Chaplin. Really old. The carvings on the cover... it was definitely not some cheap trinket."

"You don't know anything about watches."

"But *you* do," Tinker said.

Chaplin shrugged. "So you want me to ask her about it?"

"No. No, that *would* make her suspicious." She started to pace, chewing on her thumbnail as she thought. "She obviously doesn't know how much it's worth, or she wouldn't have left it out."

"Or it's not worth anything."

Tinker shook her head. "I might not know the manufacturer's name or things like that, but I know a piece of finery when I see it. That watch is money."

Chaplin tilted her head to one side. "So? What does that have to do with us? You're not thinking of stealing her watch."

Tinker didn't answer, didn't look at her.

"We don't work like that."

"You don't have to tell me how we work," Tinker said softly, then raised her voice. "Once again, *I'm* the one who taught *you* those rules."

"So you get to break them whenever you want?"

Tinker sighed and began to pace. "We're not actually stealing anything from her. Just an old watch that she clearly doesn't even think about. It's gathering dust on a shelf. We're... we're liberating it. Her life goes on the same as it always has. The same as it would if we'd never shown up. The only difference will be that we're not leaving money on the table."

"Why are you even considering this? We've already done great in Albuquerque, and the revival isn't even here yet. If we had to leave tomorrow, we'll still leave on a high. We don't have to pick some poor woman's pocket–"

"We're hardly picking her pocket. We're paying her to rent this place. So she comes out on top, too."

"Except whatever money we get for the watch is rightfully hers. If we keep it–"

"She'll never know!"

"She's a good person."

Tinker grabbed one of the empty jars off the counter and threw it at the wall. "So what!" she shouted as it shattered. "God, do you really think it makes a difference? Because I'll tell you, the past few years, I've been caring less and less. Looking into potential marks is a waste of time because if you look hard enough, they all deserve it. Everyone. Everybody. There is no one out there who isn't greedy, deep down. If we scratch the surface on Miss Sophia in there, how long do you think it would take before we found something that made it okay to take her stupid watch?"

Chaplin, stunned to silence by the broken jar, had slowly shifted to quiet rage during Tinker's speech. Her mouth was set in a firm line, and she lowered her arms to her sides.

"I'm not talking about taking food out of anyone's mouth here, Penny. She's going to have her own windfall."

Chaplin walked to the armchair and sat down. "You know, none of this matters if the watch ends up being worthless. I can ask to look at it~"

"No," Tinker said. "We cannot draw attention to it."

Chaplin stared at Tinker. "You want me to break in."

"Just to take a look at it. You can see if it's worth the effort before we make any other decisions."

"This is insane."

"No more insane than any of our other jobs."

Chaplin said, "This is straight theft, Tinker. No middle ground, no artistry, this is just taking something that isn't ours and selling it. You're honestly okay with it?"

"I'm tired, Penny. I'm tired of hoping the people we find to be too good for us to go after, but they never are. When was the last time someone passed muster?"

"Here!" Chaplin said. "Right now! Sophia passes. You're the one moving the bar."

"You can't know that. Not from one conversation over dinner."

Chaplin put her elbows on her knees. "Okay, then. I'll make you a deal. I'll go into the house after she's asleep and look at the watch. I'll see if it's even worth considering. And if it is, you won't make a move until the revival gets here. We won't grab the watch until we're on the way out of town."

Tinker considered the deal, then nodded. "We're going to be sticking around that long anyway. It would mean less chance for her to notice it missing."

"But I get the week to get to know her better. If I decide she's worthy, we leave it behind. And we tell her that it's worth something."

Tinker considered arguing further, but it seemed like a good enough compromise. She truly believed her cynical view that everyone, if you dug enough, had something dark in their closet.

"Fine. But I promise you, Chaplin, you're only setting yourself up to be disappointed."

Chaplin stood up and held out her hand. "I'm not going to count my chickens. But I have a good feeling about her."

Tinker clasped Chaplin's hand.

Whatever the outcome of the experiment was, whether the watch ended up being valuable or not, she knew that they had just crossed a line in their partnership. It didn't matter if her cynicism was right or if Chaplin's optimism would pay off, but either way, things were going to be different going forward.

INTERLUDE

PHILADELPHIA
Saturday September 21, 1940
"It seems people like to hit you."

"How would you know that?" Chaplin asked, still massaging her jaw.

Tinker gestured at the side of Chaplin's head. "Bit of cauliflower to the ear, nose is a little out of joint, healed scar on your lip. I could keep going…"

"Spare me."

Chaplin looked at this strange older woman who had just saved her from losing a finger. They had finally stopped running when they crossed the train tracks. Chaplin explained she liked to stay close to the railroad so she could make a hasty retreat. She was squatting in an empty storefront not far from where Tinker offered to buy her a drink.

"So why'd you get involved? They could have decided to chop off my finger anyway and just gone after you for sticking your nose where it didn't belong."

"Someone helped me out once. I figured helping you was a way of honoring her memory." Tinker brought her glass up, took a long drink, and licked her lips as she sat it down. "I said you needed to get better. But I know how hard that can be when you have to run full-speed just to get through a day-to-day. So I'm going to help you."

Chaplin narrowed her eyes. "Help me how?"

"You said you'd been on the road alone for ten years. And you stay close to the tracks because you jump a train when a town gets too hot?"

Chaplin didn't answer, which was answer enough.

Tinker said, "I have a truck. Tomorrow, you're leaving with me. I'll give you a place to stay, show you a few tricks that can fill your pockets enough to give you a cushion. You'll never be set for life. Hell, sometimes you'll be lucky if you can take a week off to just relax. But it's more solid than anything you're likely to find. No more worrying about one bad night. And if you listen to me and pay attention to what I say, eventually you'll be good enough that drunk bastards won't threaten to cut off your fingers."

Chaplin said, "Can I think about it?"

Tinker chuckled and nodded. "Yeah, Penny Chaplin. You go think about it." She pulled a napkin close. She stood up to look over the bar, found the bartender's pencil, and retrieved it for herself. "Be at this address tomorrow morning at six o'clock if you want to take me up on the offer. If you're not there, I'll just move on without you, no hard feelings."

"Six AM?" She looked at the clock. "That's not even four hours from now."

Tinker was already off the stool, her hat once again shading her eyes. "Then I suppose you should get back to wherever you're squatting if you want to get packed. See you tomorrow, Penny Chaplin." She flicked her finger on the hat brim. "Or not. The choice is yours."

Chaplin twisted on the stool to watch her go. She knew that this was potentially the last time she would see her mysterious savior, and she wanted to lock the memory in. Tinker stopped just outside the bar outlined by a streetlight. The glass of the bar door was wavy with age and covered with smudges and stains from god-knew-what. It created a filter that made the other woman seem unearthly, not real. She adjusted her collar, looked both ways, then crossed the street. Eventually she disappeared into the darkness.

When she left the bar, she didn't go home. She walked to the Schuylkill River and listened to the water until the sky got bright enough to see it. She'd been on her own for ten years since she left New York. She couldn't imagine working with a partner. Relying on someone else. But sometimes it was just as hard to imagine herself continuing the way she'd been going for another year. It had to end sometime, and Tinker was offering to let her end it on her own terms. And would it really be ending, or just evolving? God knew her current approach wasn't working.

"Just one bad night," she muttered to herself.

She kicked a rock into the river and took out the napkin. She waited until she could read the address, then started walking in that direction.

Tinker was sitting sideways in the driver seat of her truck, door open and feet dangling. She was eating some kind of egg sandwich, and the smell made Chaplin's stomach rumble. She looked up when Chaplin started walking toward her across the parking lot.

"No luggage?" Tinker asked.

She had a few things back where she'd been squatting, but nothing worth going back for. Nothing she wanted weighing her down.

"I travel light," she said.

Chaplin walked around the truck and opened the passenger door. A brown paper bag was sitting on the seat. The smell told her another breakfast sandwich was inside. She looked at Tinker, who was wiping the crumbs from her hands. She saw Chaplin staring at the bag and nodded at it.

"Did you already have breakfast?"

"I..." She shook her head. "No, not yet."

"Go ahead. I got that from a place called Doc's. It's the one thing I'll regret about leaving Philly. That place had the best everything."

Chaplin got in the truck and put the bag on her lap. She didn't want to seem too eager to tear into it, but her stomach was really roiling now.

"You have a preference for where we go from here?" Tinker asked.

"Not east."

Tinker nodded, apparently not requiring an explanation. "I was heading west anyway. Let's see what's out there, Penny Chaplin."

Chapter Seven

ALBUQUERQUE
Thursday July 12, 1945

Chaplin moved a chair from the dinner table to the window where she could keep an eye on the main house without being seen. She planned to watch until the lights went out, then wait an hour or so to make sure Sophia was asleep before she made her move.

Sophia had kept the kitchen window open and was currently cleaning the stove. She looked happy enough, smiling through the chore. She moved her hips and her head in a way that made Chaplin think she'd put on a record, or maybe she was just humming to herself. Either way, sometimes her lips were moving when she faced the window.

Chaplin felt worse than she ever had before a job, if she could even consider this a job. She didn't want to do it. And she was shocked at how insistent Tinker was that they go through with it. Sophia was a nice lady. She didn't really care what she learned about the watch, or how much it might be worth. Stealing from Sophia, even if she never found out about it, would make Chaplin feel like a villain. She knew they were thieves. She wasn't lying to herself about that. But she'd always believed in Tinker's rule that they only targeted bad people. The sort of people who would rob from someone else given the chance.

Over dinner, she'd learned that Sophia worked as a bank teller in Sacramento, which was the place she actually called home. She had moved to Albuquerque to take care of her mother in the late stages of an illness - "You don't want to hear the gory details, but we knew the end was coming for a long time. I've processed it." After her mother passed, she was free to leave and resume her old life in California, but she chose to stay to finish wrapping up her mother's affairs. "And there's a bit of, I don't know, settling in that I have to overcome. I got comfortable here. The idea of packing up all over again makes me tired, even if it is just to go home." She had found a new bank teller job in Albuquerque. Just temporary, she insisted, just as long as she was staying in town. She couldn't play the piano in the living room, but she did like to sing.

Chaplin watched Sophia prove her love of singing as she finished the dishes Tinker had started washing. She wished she could hear through the glass. It didn't matter if Sophia was any good or if she was terrible. Singing like this, with only dirty dishes to hear, was all about the heart and passion.

While she waited for Sophia to go to bed, she turned and looked at the closed bedroom door. She couldn't understand why Tinker was suddenly throwing Rule One out the window. They both knew what it was like to be broke and struggling, and they'd always agreed anyone they stole from had to meet certain qualifications. When they sold their elixir at revival shows, they were always on the lookout for people with worn-out shoes or threadbare shirts. It didn't take much slight of hand to return the money they'd just been paid, slipping it into a pocket as the customer walked away. It had always been their single unbreakable rule: don't take from anyone who couldn't afford to lose it.

Sophia seemed to be doing well enough. So technically she might have been an appropriate target. But she was a good person. She wasn't tricking anyone, she wasn't a thief, she wasn't greedy. Tinker was acting like the greedy one in this situation.

The light in the kitchen went out. Chaplin peeked around the curtain, then checked her watch. Years on the road had given her an uncanny internal clock, and she trusted herself to close her eyes for an hour and a half without accidentally waking up to find it was morning. She crossed her arms over her chest, put her chin to her chest, and closed her eyes.

Exactly ninety minutes later, she sat up straighter and peeked out the window. Her travels had also taught her how to be ready to move in an instant upon waking. She checked the house to make sure the lights were still out before she left.

The kitchen door was locked, but she was able to make quick and quiet work of it without breaking the mechanism. She slipped inside and stood next to the counter for a long moment to listen. The house was silent and still, every room she could see pitch black. The living room window was a bit brighter than everything else, moonglow passing through the curtains, just enough light for her eyes to adjust after a few seconds.

She crossed through the kitchen as quickly as she dared, careful not to bump the table or chairs. She had to drop into a crouch when she entered the living room so the furniture would be silhouetted against the window. She plotted her path and made her way to the bookshelf Tinker had described. She looked down the hall one more time, then took the flashlight from her pocket. She used the light to find the watch, moving close to the wall so her body would block the light from filling the room.

Chaplin knew watches. There was no real reason for it, no formal schooling, but she'd spent a decade jumping trains as her sole form of travel. Railroad men had watches and she found them interesting. Sometimes she struck up conversations with them, and they were proud of their watches. They talked about mundane things that made their watch fancier than the next guy's, and pretty soon she had a working knowledge of the market.

First she held it up to her ear. A series of quiet pings told her the watch was still running. Nothing else mattered without that fact. She checked the side and discovered it needed a key to wind and set. That was a good sign it was older. The case was very finely engraved, and she ran her fingers over the design. Gorgeous. It looked like gold, but the flashlight could have been playing tricks on her eyes. But it *was* heavy on her palm. Another good sign. She flipped it over to look at the company name.

An hourglass with wings.

Longines.

"Holy smokes," she whispered.

She was holding a Swiss watch that had probably been made during the Civil War. She was still trying to process what her next step should be when the living room filled with light from the hallway.

Her heart leapt into her throat. She turned off the flashlight, pressed the watch against her hip, and turned to see Sophia standing at the threshold to the living room. She was backlit by the hall light, the silhouette of her body visible through her nightgown. Her hair was down and the bangs nearly obscured her eyes. Chaplin swallowed hard.

"Sophia," she said. "I was getting ready for bed when I realized I'd lost a cufflink. I didn't want to bother you so I–"

Sophia shuffled toward the kitchen. There was something off about her movements. The slump of her shoulders and the dragging of her feet. It was almost like someone had grabbed the bodice of her nightgown and was pulling her along. Chaplin pressed her lips together and watched as Sophia went into the kitchen and turned on the light over the stove. She put the watch back on the bookshelf and followed.

It was just like what she'd spied the other night. Sophia was moving like an actor in a pantomime, going through the motions of making a meal without actually producing anything. She murmured under her breath a few times but none of the sounds formed into actual words that Chaplin could make out. Then she started to hum. Softly, building a melody as she moved an invisible pan over the unlit stove.

Chaplin stayed on the far side of the room from her. The shadows wouldn't do much to obscure her from someone who was actually awake, but she had the feeling it would work in this situation. As long as she didn't make any noise or step into the light, she thought she would be safe.

Sophia said, "Okay now." She stood still, sighed heavily, then began humming again. She stood motionless in front of the stove for almost three full minutes. Then she nodded, said, "That's fine," and turned off the light. Chaplin pressed her back harder against the wall, but Sophia didn't even look in her direction. She walked back to the hall and disappeared around the corner. A few seconds later, the light went out, and the house was once more silent and dark.

"What in the blazes," she whispered.

She waited for ten minutes before she risked making any noise. When she did go to the door, she took every step as quietly as possible. She pulled open the door, twisted the lock, and closed it behind her. She crossed the space between the houses in long strides, staying on the balls of her feet to minimize impact on the stones. When she got back to the guest house and opened the door just wide enough to get inside and shut it behind her.

Tinker was sitting on the couch in her undershirt and slacks. She stood up when Chaplin burst into the house.

"I heard you leave," she said. "I was watching through the window. When the light came on... how did you keep from being seen?"

"She wasn't really awake." Now that she'd escaped without being caught, the adrenaline was fading. She was shaking and sweating now, and it felt as if her heart had swelled to fill her whole chest. She tugged at the collar of her T-shirt, suddenly too tight. "Sleepwalking, I think."

"That's a real thing?" Tinker said. "I thought that was only in books and plays and stuff."

Chaplin shrugged. "Queerest thing I've ever seen. Unsettling." She shivered and started for the bathroom. She wanted to splash some cold water on her face.

Tinker stopped her. "Did you see the watch?"

Chaplin sighed. "Longines. Swiss. Probably from the 1860s or '70s."

"Gold?"

"From the weight, I'd say yeah."

Tinker's face lit up. "So... what do we do now?"

That was the big question. Chaplin wished she had any sort of answer for her.

INTERLUDE

BALTIMORE
Monday September 23, 1940

Tinker and Chaplin sat next to each other on a bench at Penn Station. Tinker had a newspaper open, mostly blocking her from being seen by the commuters rushing back and forth. Chaplin had her hands laced together between her knees, her right leg bobbing up and down nervously as she twisted her neck left and right to watch everyone who passed by. Tinker ignored the ants in her pants for twenty minutes before she finally broke her silence.

"You're acting like you've never done this before."

"I have."

"I know." Tinker looked at her. "So why are you acting like you're fresh off the farm? Just relax. Half the reason people get caught is because they act guilty. You haven't even done anything and you're acting like you have the crown jewels in your back pocket. Just keep calm and act like you're a normal person waiting for a train. Don't give anyone a reason to suspect you."

Chaplin said, "I've been doing stuff like this for ten years."

"And I'm shocked you still have all your fingers," Tinker said. "How much of that ten years have you spent behind bars?"

"Jail isn't so bad," Chaplin said. "Soft bed and a guaranteed meal. Sometimes I'm glad to get caught. It's like a vacation."

Tinker shook her paper, folding it to read the next page. "Well, I disagree. If I never see another jail cell, it will be too soon. And if you're going to be tagging along with me, you're risking *my* freedom as well as yours. So before we do anything, I'm going to find out how reliable you are. Fair enough?"

"Fair enough."

They watched people passing by for a few more minutes. Tinker had given Chaplin the mission of choosing their target, and she didn't want to fail at the very first rudimentary part of the job. She wanted to be absolutely sure she chose correctly.

She was getting desperate when she saw the man at the shoeshine stand. Finely tailored suit, a pocket square that matched his tie, salt-and-pepper hair that was perfectly parted as if he'd done it with a straight razor. He had a thin mustache running along his top lip. It was the type of grooming that only a man with time on his hands could maintain. When he cupped his hands around a match to light it, she saw that his fingernails shone in the dim train station light.

Even without all those signs, she would have chosen him for the simple fact that, when he stood up, he left his payment on the chair instead of handing it to the shoeshine. The young man had to rise from his crouch to collect the coins. Judging from the look he gave the back of his customer's head, there hadn't been a tip involved.

"Him," Chaplin said.

"Well, don't let him get away."

Tinker folded her newspaper and stood up. She went right, away from the target. Chaplin went left, directly toward him. She kept her eyes cast down as she passed him. Her hands were in her pockets, elbows out just slightly. She almost bumped into him, twisting at her waist just enough to avoid a collision since he didn't make an attempt to change his stride. She walked two more steps, then removed a wallet from her pocket and dropped into a crouch.

"Hey, mister," she said.

He glanced back at her, slowing when he saw she was holding a wallet out to him. "I think you dropped this."

The man touched his breast pocket. The mask fell back over his face as he gave a quick negative shake of his head.

"Not mine."

"Oh... Sorry for–"

He was already walking away with his back to her. Tinker had been watching, using Chaplin's ruse to discover where he was keeping his billfold, and she started walking toward him. She carried herself the same way Chaplin had, the main difference being that she didn't move to avoid him. They collided hard enough that Tinker had to take a step back, resting her hand briefly on his chest as if he had simply materialized in front of her.

"Oh gosh, I'm so sorry."

"Watch where you're going next time," he barked. He continued muttering under his breath as he stormed out of the station.

Chaplin and Tinker quickly passed through the station to exit at the opposite end. They waited until they were a fair distance before they stopped long enough to check their haul.

"Twenty-three dollars," Tinker said, handing Chaplin the ten-dollar bill. "Not bad for a morning's work. And that's another reason we only go after people like that." They started walking back to where they'd parked. "First, it's just a lot more satisfying to ruin a jerk's day. When people like that lose twenty-three dollars, it's annoying and inconveniencing. But to people like... her..."

She pointed to a woman carrying a heavy grocery bag down the opposite side of the street.

"To her, losing twenty-three dollars means her family might not eat this week. But the main reason, the practical reason, is because people like that just have more money on them at any given time. If I was soulless and tried to steal from that woman, I'd probably get fifty cents. Not worth the effort, and not worth the bad feelings I'd have about it afterward."

Chaplin shrugged. "Works for me. I wouldn't feel good about grabbing from her anyway. So I did good?"

Tinker let the question hang between them for a few beats before she smiled and dipped her chin in a nod.

"Yeah, kid, you did good. So I guess I'll let you stick around for now. Until you get annoying or become a liability."

Chaplin grinned and stuck her hands into her pockets. "So do I get to know your real name?"

Tinker laughed. "What makes you think Tinker isn't my real name?" She laughed again when she saw Chaplin's pointed look. "Fair enough. How about you? Is Penny Chaplin *your* real name?"

"No. I decided I didn't want to carry around my father's surname anymore. If I'm leaving my old self behind, might as well drop all the baggage, right? So for a while I wasn't anyone. No name. And then one night I broke into this old nickelodeon theatre to get out of the rain. There was this big advertisement on the wall for *City Lights*. Tickets were one cent. And there was a big banner underneath it." She held her hands up to frame it in the air. "CHAPLIN. PENNY. I figured, if I had to have a new name, why not choose one that had been up in lights?"

Tinker grinned and nodded. "Logical. I like it. And I like Chaplin. He's a good actor, even if he does look like that little dictator."

"That's part of why I took his name. Reclaiming it. Getting it away from the lookalike."

"So. If I asked you what name you left behind, just because I was curious about it..."

Chaplin nodded. "I get it. You're Tinker. Just Tinker. That's enough for me."

"Maybe one day I'll tell you. But it's not going to be today."

"Fair. Tinker's a fine name anyway."

"I'm so glad you approve, Miss Chaplin."

Tinker looked over her shoulder to make sure the man wasn't chasing them down. Content they'd gotten away with it, she checked to make sure everything had been transferred from the wallet. The next sewer grate they passed, she dumped the empty wallet into the gap without breaking stride.

"So you've been at the mercy of trains for a long time," Tinker said. "I think it's only fair you get to decide where we go now."

Chaplin raised her eyebrows and rubbed her chin thoughtfully. "Anywhere I want?"

"Well, you saw my truck. Anywhere you think it can reach."

"West," Chaplin said. "Let's just head west... see what we see."

"I've heard worse plans," Tinker said. "West it is."

CHAPTER EIGHT

ALBUQUERQUE
Thursday July 12, 1945

"So you said she was just wandering around the kitchen?"

"It looked like she was pretending to cook a meal," Chaplin said. "And I don't think she was asleep. But she definitely wasn't awake, either."

"Creepy."

Tinker was at the living room window, standing off to one side where she wouldn't be seen. She was holding a bowl of cereal and eating it as she watched Sophia through the curtain. She had been talking about the sleepwalking incident since she came out of the bedroom. Chaplin had spent the night on the couch since it felt like they needed a little distance between them after the argument over what to do with the watch. Now she wasn't sure if Tinker really wanted to figure out the mystery or if it was just a convenient distraction.

"We need to talk about the watch."

"I'd rather talk about the lady sleepwalking all over her house."

Chaplin leaned back in her chair. She was eating her buttered toast at the dinner table. "Are you going to stand by the deal we made last night? No moving on the watch until after the revival?"

"It would be stupid to do it any other way." Tinker walked back to the kitchen. "If she notices it missing, the new people in her guest house would be the first people she suspects."

"Okay. Then let me prove that she's a terrible target."

Tinker sighed.

"I know. Suddenly you don't give a shit. I'm not going to try to figure that out right now. But we're here through the weekend. Give me some time to get to know her. Maybe we don't have to throw away our rules for a stupid watch. Maybe there's some reason that will make me okay with taking it. Maybe she was a bad daughter, or she's cutting her siblings out of some inheritance, or..." She waved her hands in the air. "Something. Anything. It's like you said last night. Apparently every apple is rotten if you dig deep enough. We have the time. Why not use it?"

"What about running more scams in town?"

"Woodman more than paid off," Chaplin said.

Tinker sat down across from her. "Fine. I guess we don't have to do anything else. We're not exactly losing any time since we're waiting for the revival to start anyway."

Chaplin nodded. "And if I don't find anything, maybe you'll come to your senses. Or at least explain yourself better."

"Don't bet on it," Tinker muttered.

"Okay. Seriously. What's going on? You've been following the same rules since Laffite educated you about them, what, thirty years ago? My entire life, you've had one rule. And now suddenly you're throwing it out the window. You expect me to think you just had a change of heart?"

"You just said you weren't going to try to figure it out."

"Well, I changed my mind! Fucking sucks, doesn't it?" Chaplin tossed her spoon into her cereal and growled at the annoying clink it made against the bowl. "I've been traveling with you for five years. I've been trying to live up to you, and your example, and now... what... I'm supposed to just accept it's different now? For no reason? I need a reason, Tinker. Anything. Even if it doesn't make sense."

For almost a minute, Tinker remained silent. Chaplin was about to give up on getting an answer when Tinker suddenly sighed, dropped her head, and stood up.

"I'm tired. I've been doing this thirty years, Penny. Can't I just be fucking tired after all that?"

Chaplin didn't have an answer for that.

The silence hung between them until Tinker suddenly slapped

her hip and went into the living room. She sat on the couch and started putting on her shoes.

"Where are you going?"

"There's not a hell of a lot to do around here if we're not going to look for other marks. And if you're going to waste the day on Sophia, there's no reason for me to lurk back here." She finished tying her shoes and stood up. "I looked up the revival in the newspaper. It's in Santa Fe tonight and tomorrow before moving down here. I might as well go up there and watch their show, get a feel for it. See if there's an opportune moment in the script where we can jump in."

Chaplin stood up. "You're just leaving?"

"You don't need me breathing down your neck. I'll go up there, stay overnight, attend the show. Then I'll come back here and we can tell each other what we found."

"Tinker..."

"What."

Chaplin sighed. "What the hell happened? Everything has been going fine. Then we showed up here and suddenly you're..."

Tinker shook her head and went to the door. "That's the problem, Penny. You think the problem started when we got here."

She left and shut the door behind her, leaving Chaplin to wonder what the hell she'd meant by that.

Sophia's car pulled back into the driveway a little after five o'clock. She had been gone most of the day, most likely at her bank job. Chaplin could never get her mind around the idea of a nine-to-five job. Going to the same place, day in and day out. It sounded mind-numbing to her. But she supposed a steady paycheck might make up for some of the monotony.

She came out to greet Sophia, their paths crossing in front of the garage. Sophia looked surprised but pleased to see her.

"How was your day?" Chaplin asked.

"Fine," Sophia said. "Just a normal day. Work. I'm a teller at First National."

Chaplin nodded. "You mentioned, yeah." She had been expecting Sophia to be carrying something. A bag of groceries, papers from work, anything she could offer to help carry inside. But Sophia was only carrying a purse, and its strap was slung across her shoulder. She tried to quickly think of a reason for her to be there.

"Have you already had dinner?"

"Oh! Um, no. But you really don't have to reciprocate. I was just going to make a sandwich or something and then hit bed early."

Chaplin shook her head, grateful for the idea. "Don't be silly. You cooked for us last night, the least I can do is repay the favor. I love to cook. It calms me down. And Edith is sick of my cooking. It would be nice to make something for someone who will actually appreciate it."

Sophia looked like she wanted to say yes, but didn't want to take advantage. "It's really sweet..."

"Self-serving, actually," Chaplin said. "I get to cook, I get to feel good about my skills, and I get to eat with someone I find very interesting and charming at the same time."

"Interesting and charming?" Sophia laughed. "Well, maybe if I keep saying no, you'll just keep on complimenting me. I could get used to that." She sighed, giving in. "You know, driving home, even the thought of making a sandwich seemed exhausting. So if you are sincerely offering to make me actual, real food for dinner, it would be ridiculous to refuse."

Chaplin grinned wide. "I would never call you ridiculous."

"Come on inside. And thank you very much."

They went inside and Sophia went to the icebox to see what was inside. "I'm afraid I'm not offering you much to work with. I probably should have stopped at the grocery store on the way home."

"I can do magic with very little," Chaplin promised, and she was telling the truth. Just one more nifty trick she'd picked up by being on her own for ten years. "Hey, you've got a lot here. Potatoes, sausages... you don't mind sharing your meat with me, do you?"

"Of course not. Consider it payment for your services."

Chaplin grinned at her, suddenly aware of the fact their arms were pressing against each other as they stared into the icebox. She cleared her throat and shifted her weight under the guise of reaching in to start taking out the ingredients she needed.

"Have you ever had toad in the hole?"

"I think I would remember something like that."

"It's great. You'll love it. Do you have any butter?"

"Yes." Sophia went to retrieve it from a covered dish. "Anything else?"

Chaplin began preparing the stove. "Flour, salt, and half a pint of milk. Water will do if you're short."

"Okay, good."

They worked in silence for a few minutes, Chaplin only speaking to give instructions. Once the meal was underway, she wiped her hands and smiled.

"Should be all set. It'll be ready in about half an hour."

Sophia nodded. "Thank you. I really do appreciate it. You're definitely going above and beyond what I expected from a tenant."

"Well, so far you've been a very good landlady. So I guess we're even."

"Would you like something to drink while the food is cooking?"

Chaplin gestured to the living room. "Actually... I was hoping that maybe I could fool around on the piano a little while you were unwinding from work. If you wanted to change clothes or take a bath or something." She ran her hand along the dusty top of the piano. "I played as a kid and I miss it like crazy. I guess I'm really just curious to see if I still remember anything from those days."

Sophia said, "Oh! That would be lovely, actually. No one has played that thing in... decades, probably. My mother tried to make me learn when I was a girl, but I never took to it." She chewed her bottom lip. "I *was* planning to take a bath when I got home. So you don't mind being left alone?"

"Not if you trust leaving me unsupervised in your house."

Sophia laughed. "I trust you. I'll just be in the other room."

Chaplin nodded. She watched Sophia leave, then looked at where the pocket watch was still resting. If she'd known how trustworthy Sophia would be, she never would have risked breaking in the night before. She pulled out the bench from underneath the piano and sank down onto it.

Sophia had cleaned up the house after the first time she'd seen it, and the piano was no longer cluttered with books and newspapers. It had still been neglected but Chaplin could sense it still wanted to be played. She stretched her fingers and held them over the keys. She took a breath, held it, and then lowered her fingers and began to play.

She hadn't planned to play a full song, but her hands seemed to take off on their own. She was halfway through the first verse of "Blue Skies" before she realized what she was playing. She smiled and hummed along with the melody, rocking her head along and tapping her foot. When she got to the chorus, she looped back to start the song properly.

Then, from the back of the house, she heard Sophia's voice join in. "Blue skies, smiling at me... nothing but blue skies do I see..."

Chaplin's hands hesitated but she quickly recovered and continued the song. She had heard the water running without realizing it, and now she tried very hard not to picture Sophia. Lounging in the bath, her hair up, eyes closed as she sang the tune. Sophia was a very lovely woman. Very lovely. And her voice was gorgeous. And the combination of the voice and her mental image made her fumble the bridge. She recovered quickly, but she heard Sophia laugh.

"I told you I was rusty!" Chaplin called.

"Your secret is safe with me. As long as you don't mind my singing voice.

"You sounded lovely."

"As did you. Please keep playing."

"Any requests?"

There was a long silence, and then Sophia said, "Keep it with Berlin. I love 'Always,' if you know it."

Chaplin had to think. She hummed the melody before she began playing the chorus. "I don't remember how it starts. But I think..." She closed her eyes and sang. "I'll be loving you, always. With a love that's true, always..."

She continued humming into the verse. Sophia was either silent or singing so quietly Chaplin couldn't hear her, but soon her voice drifted down the hall again.

"Not for just an hour. Not for just a day. Not for just a year..."

Chaplin sang, "Always," in harmony with her.

She kept playing the song, surprised at how well her fingers remembered how to move over the keys. Every other time she'd considered playing again, she was terrified of flashbacks to starched dresses and bobby pins hurting her hair, sitting up so straight that it hurt her back. She always kept her head down so she could watch her fingers. She couldn't mess up, not in God's house, not playing God's songs. Her father would have been absolutely furious if she'd fumbled on a hymn.

And now look at her. She had fumbled and it had been fine. Sophia had laughed, the song had continued, and that was it. How freeing that was. To know she didn't have to be perfect as long as the heart of the music remained.

She played faster, bobbing her head to the rhythm, tapping her foot. She finished 'Always' and moved into something faster, jazzier.

Chaplin got lost in the music, playing with her eyes closed, and she didn't realize how long she'd been playing until she was startled by Sophia sliding onto the bench next to her. She was wearing a robe that was cinched tight enough that it was hard to tell if she was wearing anything underneath. But when she repositioned, it fell away to reveal a sliver of bare thigh.

Chaplin tensed but quickly recovered. She scooted over and smiled. "Do you know any duets?"

"I barely know how to play," Sophia said. "But, um... well. There's one song..." She laughed, shook her head, and then began to play 'The Celebrated Chop Waltz.'

Chaplin laughed as well and nodded. "Just because it's common doesn't mean it's easy. Very good."

"You're kind. Thank you." She breathed in and looked toward the kitchen. "Dinner smells fantastic."

"I should check on it, actually."

She got up and went into the kitchen. Sophia followed.

"Is your sister going to be joining us?"

Tinker was the absolute last thing Chaplin wanted to talk about. She shook her head as she peered into the oven. "She had something she needed to do in Santa Fe. Boring bank stuff." She remembered Sophia was a teller. "Oh. No offense."

"None taken. Banking is very, very boring. I only took the job because it was available and I didn't think I would be staying long. But a few weeks turn into a few months and then..." She shrugged. "I shouldn't dismiss it like that. It's a steady paycheck, and I'm very lucky to have it."

"There's nothing wrong with wanting more for yourself."

Sophia made a quiet noise of agreement and nodded. She looked at the pan Chaplin had taken from the oven.

"Wow! That looks as good as it smells."

"I'll serve it up."

"Excellent. I'll go get dressed and be right back."

Chaplin nodded and watched her leave, then began searching the kitchen for plates.

Sophia returned in a lightweight white dress covered with small yellow flowers. Her hair was pinned back so it wouldn't fall in her face, but a few strands had fallen loose anyway. She took glasses from the cupboard and offered Chaplin her choice of milk, water, or tea. Chaplin took water and Sophia did the same, pouring from the tap. She smiled as she took her seat at the table, and Chaplin sat to her right.

"May I ask you something that might be personal?" Chaplin asked. "You don't have to answer."

"Only if I can ask you something in return."

Chaplin hesitated briefly and then nodded. Sophia gestured for her to go first. "Last night, I couldn't sleep. I happened to notice the lights were on over here, so I looked out. You were in the kitchen. It looked like you were... I don't know. Cooking? I didn't notice the time, but it seemed very early."

"Last night?" Sophia looked genuinely confused. "I went straight to bed. The sun was up when I made breakfast, so I never turned on the lights."

Chaplin searched her face for tell-tale signs she was lying, but found nothing. She'd known liars before. She'd known *great* liars, and she'd spent the past five years on the road with Tinker. She could spot a tell from a mile away. Sophia legitimately didn't know what she was talking about.

"Maybe it was a dream," Sophia suggested.

"Maybe." Chaplin decided to drop it. "Okay. Turnabout is fair play. I owe you a personal question."

Sophia smiled slyly. "I think I'll hold onto it. Really think about what I want to ask."

"Uh-oh." Chaplin laughed. "I'm dealing with a professional here."

"I don't throw away golden geese," Sophia said.

"No, I respect it. I'll be prepared."

"You'd better be." Sophia took a bite of her food, then pointed at the plate with her fork. "This is magnificent, by the way. I can't imagine what you'd be capable of without rationing."

Chaplin shrugged. "I've always been rationed, in a way. Very strict upbringing."

"Oh? You don't have to tell me if you don't want to."

"No, it's fine. And I won't make you burn your question on this." Chaplin was confused by her willingness to tell the truth instead of a well-worn lie. "My father was a pastor. Small-town church. He was the kind of church leader who believed it was a lifestyle, not a job. He was a representative of God on Earth and it was his duty to act like a proper disciple. And his family was expected to follow suit."

"That must have been hard growing up that way."

"It was the only life I knew," Chaplin said. "So I was a good girl. Perfect posture. Learned piano so I could play at church every Sunday."

"And your sister?"

Sister...? Shit, my sister. Chaplin was thrown by the question, but she thankfully recovered before she gave herself away. She hated being thrown. She was better than that. "She was older. So of course she was expected to marry and start a family of her own as quickly as possible."

Sophia nodded knowingly. "I understand. I had the same pressure growing up. I assume she's the one who got you out of there."

Chaplin took a bite so she could buy some time. There were multiple routes she could take, but once she said the words, she couldn't walk it back. She could either continue to build the lie she and Tinker had started the other day, or she could break off on a new path. Sophia was already suspicious about the claim they were sisters. If that suspicion festered and grew, she might start digging into their story. Curiosity could be a dangerous thing.

So the obvious course of action was to give her a confession.

"Edith isn't really my sister."

Sophia allowed herself a little smile. "I kind of suspected, if I'm honest. Age gaps like that aren't unheard-of for siblings, but it was a little odd."

"We get away with it about half the time," Chaplin said. "The truth is... I was the one being pushed to get married young. My father found the perfect candidate. The son of a prominent businessman in our town. Neither of us were old enough to get married yet, but Daddy wanted to do a ceremony swearing myself to him."

"Oh goodness." Sophia shook her head. "That is one reason I ran far and fast away from any kind of religion as soon as I could. My mother used to drag us to church and Sunday school every week. That was one reason I moved so far away. So she couldn't guilt me into going even after I became an adult. It's strange how much church dictates pretty much everyone's life. We either grow up and embrace it, or we escape and never, ever look back."

"Here's to getting away," Chaplin said, raising her glass.

"And staying gone," Sophia said, clinking her glass against Chaplin's.

CHAPTER NINE

SANTA FE

Thursday July 12, 1945

Tinker was too furious to think for the first twenty minutes of the drive. She had left without saying goodbye to Chaplin. It wasn't unheard of for them to spend time apart. Sometimes there were lulls like this and it was beneficial for them to split up. She was gathering information, useful data that could help them out when the revival got the Albuquerque. But she still stared at the long stretch of road ahead of her and fought against the feeling that she was running away.

She didn't even really *want* that stupid watch. She and Chaplin had a good cushion of cash from Oklahoma that could get them all the way to California if they wanted. Los Angeles, San Francisco, maybe even all the way up to Sacramento, or down to cross the border into Mexico. The gold rush was still happening if you knew where to look, and Tinker had always had a nose for opportunities to line her pockets. The future was looking bright and shiny.

So why was she so insistent about the stupid watch? Chaplin didn't want to take it. Chaplin liked Sophia. Fine. That shouldn't matter. She'd never needed a reason in the past. If one of them had a bad feeling about a job, they didn't do it. No explanations needed. Just a shake of the head and the curtain was drawn. They had lost money in a lot of card games because something didn't smell right. They'd walked away from a bag full of cash because the person offering seemed off. It had kept them alive and rich as they crossed the lower half of the country.

Why wasn't Chaplin's word good enough now?

Because you want to take something from Sophia.

She clenched her jaw. It was Laffite's voice in her head, just as it had been for most of her life. The old woman might as well have been sitting beside her in the truck. Her conscience, her better judgement, the angel on her shoulder.

You saw how Chaplin looked at her at dinner. How Sophia smiled back.

"Nothing's happening."

And you left them all alone today. What do you think is happening back there?

Tinker shook her head as if that would clear the cobwebs. "Shut up. I don't care what's happening. It doesn't involve me. If Chaplin finds comfort back there, fine. That's just fine. We've both had our fun before. It doesn't mean anything. Never means anything."

Never?

She had a flash of an Oklahoma motel room. Despite the sweltering temperatures inside the truck, goosebumps rose on Tinker's arms. She ran her thumbs over the steering wheel. It was sticky from the sun and reminded her she was in the desert, not a snowstorm. She wasn't in a freezing hotel room. Chaplin wasn't between her legs...

Her eyes had closed in the throes of the memory and she opened them to find she had drifted into the oncoming lane. "Damn it," she hissed, swerving back over he lines. Luckily no one was coming in either direction, but the last thing she needed was to drive into the scrub and wreck the truck. If she blew a tire she could change it. If she blew more than one... well, that would be a very long walk for help.

You want to take something from Sophia before she takes Chaplin from you.

"I thought I told you to shut up."

She stared at the road until her mentor's voice faded, replaced by the hum of tires on the road. She hummed along with it and focused on keeping straight until the desert started giving way to civilization. She pulled off the road at a rest stop and pulled her bag from underneath the truck's seat. She took it into the ladies room and, after checking to make sure she was alone, started to transform herself into someone else.

It was second nature to her at this point. Other women could apply makeup on autopilot and look beautiful every time. Tinker knew how to use the bare minimum of materials. The trick was to not overdo it. Anyone could disguise themselves with a wig and fake teeth and big sunglasses. To truly disguise yourself, you had to create a whole new person.

Contouring could change her cheekbones, widen her lips, change the shape of her eyes. She dug through her bag until she found an onion and cut thin slices from it. These would go into her pockets, then under her thumbnails. A quick sniff would make her eyes water just enough that they became puffy. She blinked at her reflection and turned her head one way, then the other. It wouldn't be enough to fool anyone long-term, but for a cursory glance in a crowd, it did the trick a hundred percent of the time.

Once her face was done, she traded her normal clothes for a baggy dress that they'd gotten from a thrift store in Arkansas the year before. It looked like it had been raided from the estate sale of someone's grandmother, but it was perfect for what she needed. Her last trick was doing up her hair, braiding and tying it so it looked half as long as usual.

When she was done she stepped back and took in the full look. She saw not a stranger looking back at her, but a woman she'd met variations of throughout the south.

"Well, hello, sweetheart," she purred, affecting her best Georgian accent. "You look younger every time I see you, and that is a fact!" She laughed a chirpy laugh, also unfamiliar to her, and returned her supplies to the bag.

By the time she got back to the truck, she decided her Santa Fe name would be Louisa Mellick. It was an unusual surname, but not so unusual as to raise eyebrows. And if anyone she introduced herself happened to know a Mellick family, it would be easy for her to just claim she came from back east and wasn't really sure if she had any relatives in the area. Most people weren't interested enough to dig much deeper than that.

On the way back to the truck, she practiced her new walk. Louise couldn't walk the same way Tinker did. Her stride would be different, less confident. Her posture would be stiffer. She would bend her knees as little as possible and avoid bending at the waist.

By the time she slid behind the wheel, she felt like she had a good handle on who she was playing.

The newspaper on the passenger seat was open to the revival advertisement. She took the map from her glove compartment and unfolded it to find the revival's address. She could have just driven around until she spotted the giant tent, but this would save time and gas.

She drove to the location and was surprised to find there was already a sizable crowd gathered in the park next to the tent. She parked a couple of blocks away - Louisa would absolutely not be driving a truck like this - and walked back to the park.

"Afternoon, ladies!" She lifted her hand toward the group of mostly women, waggling her fingers in greeting.

The women turned to look at her with polite curiosity. One of them held a hand over her eyes to block the sun as she tried to determine if the new arrival was someone she knew.

"My name is Louisa. Louisa Mellick. I was just passing on through when I stopped to get myself some lunch, and I saw an announcement in the newspaper about this wonderful event. I knew I couldn't live with myself if I missed it." She sighed and looked up at the tent as if it was a holy temple. "It seemed like a sign. Like I needed to be here. And I never ignore a sign from the Lord."

One of the women offered a slow, still-wary smile. "Well, aren't you something, dear. My name is Mildred. We're with the First Methodist of Santa Fe. We're here setting up in preparation for tonight's meeting. Would you like to lend a hand?"

"Oh my, yes. I'd absolutely love to be useful." Tinker laughed and pressed her hand to her chest. "You know what they say about idle hands! Just point me where I can help."

She was assigned to set up chairs inside the tent with two other women, who were introduced as Laura and Mary. The stage was already up, with risers at the back where a local choir would likely be stationed. She chatted with the women and, in getting to know them, got an idea of what kind of people were going to attend the revival that night. She could think of a few cons she could run by herself, since she was there. It wasn't like she really needed the money, and it would feel strange working without Chaplin to watch her back. But she'd done a few games alone before Chaplin came along. And if things kept going the way they were, she might be doing them alone again soon.

"You look absolutely lost in your mind, dear," one of the local women said.

Tinker smiled and waved away her concern. "Oh, these things always put me in a contemplative mood. You know how it is. You can't wash away your sins and regrets unless you acknowledge them."

"Now that is the truth," the other local woman said.

"The God's honest truth," her friend added.

"Mm-hmm," Tinker said, nodding emphatically. "I don't feel like I took time out of my trip to be here. I feel like I'm here because this is where I was guided."

Both Mary and Laura loved that, nodding and agreeing loudly. And just like that, Tinker had earned their trust. She could take them for all the money in their purses now without breaking a sweat. She could convince them to hand over their bracelets, necklaces, rings, and they would feel like saints for doing it. She didn't need their things or their cash. She didn't even particularly want it, but she could. It was there for the taking.

After almost three decades of doing this, she barely felt the thrill anymore. Part of what she'd told Chaplin had been true. She really did believe most people, deep down, were bad and greedy. But she also believed that anyone who fell for their ridiculous lies deserved to lose their money. They sold colored water. They spoke with confidence and waved around identification that they had crafted so recently that the ink was sometimes still wet.

And people kept giving them money. Throwing it at them, insisting they take it. So why were they drawing some arbitrary line? People were gullible. Losing money would be a learning experience for them, and she and Chaplin could stop wasting time looking for the "right" targets.

"Oh, oh!" Mary slapped Laura's arm rapidly, then pointed. "Look! The reverend is here!"

Tinker glanced over her shoulder because she assumed Louisa would be intrigued. When she saw who was crossing the grass toward them, she snapped upright and pressed down on the ground with both feet to fight the urge to flee.

Reverend Ephraim "Rumble" Riggs was less than fifty yards away from her, outside the tent, stopped to speak with other members of Laura and Mary's church.

"This isn't…" She coughed and cleared her throat, furrowed her brow. She couldn't remember what accent she was supposed to be using. "I-I know of him, heard the name, of course, and I didn't think this was one of his revivals..."

"No, we're very lucky." Mary gasped and put her hand to her chest. "Oh goodness. I didn't mean to say lucky! The usual reverend fell ill in Kansas. He had to be hospitalized. Fortunately, Reverend Riggs was available to substitute for him. All very last minute."

"The Lord works in mysterious ways." Laura patted Mary's shoulder. "And I am sure He understands what you meant when you said 'lucky.'"

Tinker's hands had gone numb. She knew exactly why Riggs had been available to take over, and it hadn't been due to God's mysterious ways.

It was because she and Chaplin had destroyed his revival.

She turned her back on Riggs and clapped a hand over her stomach. "Oh, can you believe it? I was so excited to get here that I just plumb forgot to have lunch."

Mary cocked her head to the side. "Didn't you say you were at lunch when you saw the advertisement in the newspaper?"

Tinker mentally kicked herself for slipping up. "Did I?" Sloppy. So damned sloppy. "I must have meant breakfast. And then I drove all the way here, I completely lost sense of time." She looked at her watch. "Yes. I meant breakfast. And then I... skipped lunch." She shook their hands as she hurried away. "I'm sorry to leave you ladies without help, but I need to go get some food before I faint and make more work for you."

She trotted from the tent before they could gather their wits enough to ask questions. She moved around the tent, keeping it between her and the reverend.

She waited until she was around the corner before she broke into a run. They had to forget about Albuquerque, forget about the watch. She had to get back, grab Chaplin, and drive west or north or south as fast as they possibly could. It didn't matter how many supplies they'd wasted on the elixir bottles, they would just leave them behind. No time to pack them. Some kind saint of thieves had given them a head start, and she wasn't going to squander a second of it.

Her mind was on possible destinations as she ran up to her truck. She thought the best plan of action would be driving as far as the truck could take them before they even thought of stopping again. No more revivals, it didn't matter what Chaplin said. Too dangerous. They would focus on quick cons, on small targets, keep their heads down.

Her brain was a second too late processing the fact the driver's side door was ajar. It was distracted by trying to process the dark shape stretched across the seat.

She realized it was Riggs' henchman Osker just before the man kicked his foot forward. The door swung outward and hit Tinker in the face. The impact sent her stumbling back. Osker climbed from the truck and left the door standing open as he closed the distance between them. She swung blindly. He ducked away and drove a fist into her gut. When she doubled over, he stepped on her leg and made her kneel, then grabbed a handful of her hair. He pulled it hard and she cried out, cursing herself for not wearing a wig.

"The Rev said it was the same truck. We all told him, 'nah, there isn't a chance they're still driving that old beater.' Get up."

He hauled her to her feet and shoved her forward. He was still holding tight to her hair. She tried to stand her ground but, after a moment of pressure, she had to either start walking or fall flat on her face. He aimed her back the way she'd come, back toward the revival tent.

"But he told me to wait. I figured I was going to terrify some innocent young mother. But I just had to settle in for a minute or two and suddenly there you are. Like a gift from heaven. If you believe in that bullshit."

"I have money."

"Not enough, darling. Keep walking."

Something warm was trickling across her upper lip. She assumed the door had cracked her in the nose hard enough to make it bleed. She reached up to wipe it away, but Osker shoved her and grabbed her wrist, yanking it back down to her side.

A massive purple-black Alfa Romeo was parked at the end of the block. It looked like an eggplant on wheels, disgusting in a way she couldn't quite articulate. A man she recognized from Riggs' 'congregation' was leaning against the front bumper. He straightened when he saw Osker approaching, confusion clear on his face as he tried to figure out what was happening.

"Vernon," Osker said. "Go tell the Rev one of his little Byrdies is back."

"Holy hell," Vernon said, then turned and ran toward the tent.

Osker roughly shoved her into the backseat of the car. She eyed the passenger door and wondered how fast she would have to move to open it and escape before Osker or Vernon could catch up with her.

"Keep thinking that way," Osker said as he got into the car behind her. "I'll break one of your kneecaps and save myself a lot of trouble."

She settled back into the leather seat. Her heartbeat was a hummingbird against her ribs. It was making her breathless.

After a few minutes of trying to settle her racing mind, the passenger door opened. Reverend Riggs slammed his beastly bulk into the seat, causing the whole car to shift under his weight. He twisted to look at her from between the seats. His lips curled away from his disgusting teeth in a wickedly pleased smile. He had grown a beard since the last time they'd seen him, white muttonchops with a gray muzzle.

"The talented Missus Driscoll," he said, his voice liquid and intimidating. "We meet again. Your father misses you, Emilie."

For the first time in decades, Tinker felt true fear.

INTERLUDE

SOUTH OF EMPORIA, KANSAS
Sunday April 9, 1944

Night had fallen during the revival, but lanterns had been brought in to make sure the interior of the tent was still bright as mid-afternoon. They had been poorly placed, however, and the bizarre shadows cast on the canvas walls gave the procession of the sick and injured look ghoulish and almost demonic as they waited for Reverend Riggs' healing touch.

The people of Emporia had endured a great deal of suffering since the war began. The men unable to fight overseas were forced to take over jobs they were unqualified for. Accidents at the food-packing were the cause of blindness, crushed hands, broken bones, and the victims were putting their faith in the massive stone of a man standing on the stage to heal the damage done to their bodies.

Chaplin's legs trembled as she stepped up onto the stage. She leaned heavily on a crutch, back bowed, head down, her face obscured by a long gray wig. Her movements were stiff due to necessity. She couldn't bend her arms or knees very far, so her stride was naturally slow and ponderous. Osker put his hand on her shoulder, gentle and warm, and guided her toward the center of the stage. She muttered her thanks to him as she shuffled her feet across the carpeted platform, her voice barely more than a whisper. Riggs loomed over her and she put on a good show of trying to stand up straight.

"My goodness, you're even larger up close!" Her voice wavered and cracked, like the words were being carried on water instead of air. The words were also obscured by the cherry tomato tucked between her teeth and cheek.

Riggs laughed, and even a few of his people joined in. "I get that all the time, believe me! Now, my dear, what is your name?"

"Gertrude," she said. "But everyone calls me Gertie."

He rested one baseball mitt hand on her shoulder, the same one Osker had touched. "I'm sure they do. I know a woman like you must be very beloved in this community."

No one in this community had ever seen her before. But none of them were rude enough to speak up, and Chaplin just pressed her lips together and nodded.

"I have been blessed with family, both blood and not."

"What a life, what a life," Riggs said. "But even the most charmed life comes with shadows, doesn't it, Gertie?"

"Amen!" someone in the line said.

"What troubles you?" Riggs said. "What in your life requires the Lord's blessing tonight?"

She swallowed hard. "My bones ache," she said, her voice cracking even more. "I can hardly move. I can't... I can't sleep at night for the pain. Lying down hurts, standing up hurts even more, I can't stand it any longer. I just need... I need... relief."

"I understand," Riggs said gently. "Let me see what I can do to help."

He placed his other hand on her opposite shoulder and then squeezed. If Chaplin really did have aching bones, she was certain his grip would have been unbearable. She clenched her teeth and cringed, bent her knees, letting out a trembling moan.

"I can feel s-something ha-happening," she said.

"That's the spirit, Gertie."

"Why does it hurt so?" she moaned.

She caught Riggs' eyes open ever so briefly, then snap shut again. "The pain is being... pulled from you. It's fighting, Gertie, but soon you will feel relief..."

Chaplin let out an unholy scream, then bent her arms. The twigs strapped between her forearm and bicep snapped with the sound of breaking bones. She dropped to her knees, and the twigs attached to her thighs and calves also snapped with equal force. The crowd screamed in horror as Chaplin writhed in manufactured pain, tears filling her eyes as her mouth twisted in agony. Riggs loomed over her, his eyes wide with surprise and fear.

"What can we do?" Riggs asked, desperation creeping into his voice.

"I-I-I need..." She kept her voice so low that only he could hear. Then she opened her eyes and let her mask slip a little. "I need a bottle of the Byrd Sisters Miraculous Spring Elixir."

Riggs furrowed his brow. Then his eyes widened as he recognized her. "*You*," he hissed.

Chaplin cried out again and grabbed the lapels of his jacket. "Please, Reverend! The pain!"

Riggs was blinded by his rage. He pulled away from her, took a step back, and swung his wrecking ball of a fist at her head.

The blow would have definitely knocked her out if it made full contact. But Chaplin had been prepared, and the idiot telegraphed his punch enough that any fool could have avoided it. She turned her head at just the right time that only his knuckles made glancing contact with her cheek. That was enough for the crowd. All they saw was a terrified, suffering old woman being punched in the face. Chaplin bit down on the cherry tomato and spit a thin stream of red juice toward the crowd. It didn't look anything like blood to anyone paying attention, but no one was taking the time to analyze the situation.

The crowd was screaming now. Some in anger, most in shock. Several men had rushed the stage and slammed into Riggs. It took four of them to push him away from Chaplin, who was already back on her feet. The tent had descended into madness and she found it very easily to weave through the crowd once she pulled off her wig and started moving like a younger woman.

She was outside in seconds, already pulling off the dress to reveal her undershirt and slacks underneath. Halfway to the truck, Tinker fell into step beside her.

"Do you think people will be talking about that tomorrow?"

"Definitely," Tinker said. "Especially if someone happened to be taking pictures that somehow made it to the newspapers."

Chaplin said, "What are the odds of that?"

Tinker held up her camera and smiled. "Maybe we'll get lucky."

Chaplin laughed and looped her arm around Tinker's.

"How was the punch?"

"No trouble," Chaplin said. "It was sloppy enough that we might as well have choreographed it. How'd it look?"

"It *looked* phenomenal. The tomato sauce won't fool anyone, but people's memories will do the heavy lifting on that for us."

Chaplin nodded. By the time the story started spreading, she was sure people would swear they'd been splattered by the blood. Maybe they would even add in a few flying teeth that had been knocked loose. *The old woman's dentures flew out of her mouth and landed at my feet!* She laughed at her own thoughts and looked back over her shoulder at the tent.

The pictures turned out perfectly. The next morning, every newspaper across Kansas showed Reverent "Rumble" Riggs punching an old woman seconds after apparently breaking every bone in her body. The fact that "Gertrude" disappeared without a trace only made Riggs look worse. People speculated that the Reverend's entourage had made her go away to avoid further scandal.

By the time Tinker and Chaplin crossed into Oklahoma, all pending revivals for Riggs and his crew had been canceled until further notice. They read a notice in the Tulsa newspaper when they stopped for breakfast and toasted each other with their orange juice for a job well done.

On that morning, it seemed like "Rumble" Riggs was a name they would never have to worry about ever again.

Chapter Ten

ALBUQUERQUE
Thursday July 12, 1945

When they finished dinner, Chaplin took the dishes to the sink and peeked out the window toward the driveway. Sophia joined her and looked as well.

"You expected your sister to be back by now?"

"I'm sure she just got caught up in business," Chaplin said.

Sophia smiled. "Sure. I understand how business can be." She turned on the faucet and added soap. "You're more than welcome to stay until she comes back."

"I wouldn't want to be an imposition."

"Absolutely not. I also understand how quiet and empty houses can be. You would be doing me a favor if you did want to stick around."

Chaplin really wanted a chance to sit quietly and think about where Tinker might be. Maybe the revival had run late, or they didn't have a show until Friday night. Maybe the truck had broken down. It might have seemed easier to get a motel room and stay in town rather than driving back and forth. There was a phone in the guest house, but neither of them had bothered to take note of the number.

So if there was no reason to wait by the phone, and no way for her to drive up to Santa Fe to find Tinker on her own, she might as well stick around. Sophia was right. Empty houses were no fun at all.

"Yeah, okay. I could play you a few more songs on the piano."

"Hah! Well, I'd hate to put you to work, but that would be lovely." She gestured at the plate Chaplin was washing. "Will doing the dishes ruin your fingers?"

"No, no, they bounce back pretty quick."

Sophia smiled. "Maybe you can give me lessons. I can cut your rent down a little to pay for them."

"I don't know if we'll be around that long, honestly." Sophia flinched at that, her eyes widening as her lips pressed together, and then just as quickly her features relaxed back to neutral. "I just don't like starting something I can't finish. I would hate to leave you in the lurch."

"That makes sense. But either way, it would still be lovely if you played something."

"Of course."

"Thank you."

Chaplin didn't want to just wash the dishes in silence, but they'd spoken about so much over the last two dinners that she didn't know what was left. But at the same time, she felt as if she barely knew the woman whose elbow kept bumping against hers. She'd left home young, came back when her mother got sick, and she had been living in the house trying to get the estate in order before she went back to her real home. She didn't explain what was taking so long, or what sort of life she'd left on pause back in Sacramento. Was there a husband? A boyfriend? How could someone just leave their whole world on ice with no idea of when they'd return?

Of course, Chaplin didn't have any experience with a life like that. A normal life with a house and a job, and people who expected you to be around. When she first left home, life on the road had seemed freeing. Roots tied people down, strapped their feet to the ground where they were born, never letting up until they finally pulled you under in a coffin.

She realized she had been scrubbing with unnecessary vigor. She glanced to her right and saw Sophia watching her, concerned but not commenting. She breathed out sharply and shook her head.

"I'm sorry."

"No, whatever you were thinking seemed important. I didn't want to interrupt."

Chaplin shrugged. "I was thinking about when we move on. Edith and me. I don't know where we're going. I never really do, and neither does she. We sort of like it that way." Sophia nodded that she understood. "But sometimes I wonder why we're so positive it's going to be better than the place we're leaving. I mean. We're not always leaving bad places."

She glanced at Sophia and then quickly away before they could make eye contact.

"Can I ask you something?" Sophia asked quietly.

"Sure."

Sophia leaned in and pressed her lips to the corner of Chaplin's mouth.

The kiss was brief, the retreat quick. She seemed to take all the air with her when she leaned back. Chaplin found it hard to draw breath. She looked at Sophia, whose cheeks were bright red.

"What... wh-what was the question?" Chaplin asked.

"I think I got my answer. I'm sorry."

She stepped away from the sink. Chaplin grabbed Sophia's hand, turned so they were facing each other, and pulled her back. Sophia made a quiet sound of happy surprise right before their lips met. Sophia pulled her hand away from Chaplin's and moved it to her hip instead. Her other hand went to the back of Chaplin's head, fingers curling in her hair. She angled her body toward Chaplin, who pulled her closer and then pinned her against the counter.

The kiss ended by an unspoken mutual agreement but they didn't move apart. Sophia brushed the backs of her fingers over Chaplin's cheeks, then brushed her thumb over her bottom lip.

"How did you know?"

"I didn't," Sophia said. "I hoped. Based on the way you dress. The way you walk." She licked her lips and shrugged. "Then you said you might not be around for long, so I thought the consequences were minimal."

"I'm glad you took the risk."

Sophia smiled nervously. She hadn't taken her eyes off Chaplin's lips. "I was also worried about... about your 'sister.'" She finally met Chaplin's gaze. "You said she wasn't really your sister. The other thought I had... I mean, the other explanation for why two women might be traveling together, living together... being okay with only one bed..."

Chaplin shook her head. "No. It's not like that. She's not... we're..." She shook her head. "You don't have to worry about her."

"Okay."

They kissed again, this time with no hesitation or holding back. Sophia moved her hands down to the waistband of Chaplin's pants, hooked her fingers in the belt loops and pulled her forward as she rolled her own hips, pressing against her. Chaplin had her hands in Sophia's hair, tugging it free from the up-do and luxuriating in how it felt as it tumbled over her fingers.

"Take me into the bedroom," Sophia said against Chaplin's mouth.

"Are you sure?"

Sophia nodded and pushed away from the counter. They held hands as they crossed through the house, leaving all the lights on in their wake. Sophia left the bedroom dark, but they didn't close the door so the hallway light spilled in. Sophia went to the bed and tossed something off the mattress onto the floor, then turned to face Chaplin.

"Have you ever done this before?" Chaplin asked, moving in close again.

"Yeah." Sophia's voice was shaky. "But it's been a long time."

"For me, too."

"Ten years," Sophia said.

Chaplin's eyes widened. "Seriously?"

Sophia nodded. Her eyes went back to Chaplin's mouth. "Kiss me..."

The last word was muffled by Chaplin complying. She pushed Sophia down onto the mattress and knelt in front of her. Sophia moved her feet apart and ran her hands through Chaplin's hair, moving it out of her face so she could look down into her eyes. Chaplin looked up at her as she pushed up the hem of Sophia's dress, baring her thighs.

"I think you've waited long enough, don't you?"

Sophia was breathing hard, visibly flushed even in the dark. "Please."

Chaplin tucked her bottom lip into her mouth, ran her tongue over her top lip. She kissed the inside of her knee, licked up the length of her thigh, moving the dress higher to clear a path for herself. Sophia kept one hand on the back of Chaplin's head and moaned in anticipation as she dropped backward on the mattress.

They shared a cigarette afterward, Sophia cradled in the crook of Chaplin's arm and staring at the ceiling. Sophia's arms and legs were like liquid. Chaplin felt as if she could pick her up with one hand to position her like a rag doll. She ran her finger down the center of Sophia's chest, gathering the sweat that shined in her cleavage, and smiled when Sophia shuddered at the touch.

"I hope that was worth waiting ten years," Chaplin said.

"It's a start."

Chaplin grinned and kissed the top of Sophia's head.

"How about you?" She craned her head up to look at Chaplin. "You said it had been a long time for you, too."

"Oh." She shook her head, trying to dismiss the question as she took another drag on the cigarette. "That doesn't matter."

Sophia chuckled. "I kind of threw you for a loop with mine, huh."

"No, no. That's a perfectly reasonable..." She coughed. "Okay. Christmas."

"Well, well. That's a nice gift."

Chaplin grinned.

Sophia was quiet for a few minutes. When she decided she wasn't going to get any further details, she started talking.

"It's one of the reasons I left Albuquerque to begin with. My mother was very, very religious. If she'd even had a hint that I was interested in women, I would have ended up..." She waved her hand toward the ceiling. "I don't know. Disappeared or something. So I just went as far as I could, to somewhere no one knew me. The downside was that Sacramento was a completely foreign country for me. I didn't have any friends, I certainly didn't trust anyone. So eventually I just went about my life and didn't think about romance."

"Huh," Chaplin said quietly.

"Hm?"

"No, it's..." She waved away the smoke. "I wasn't thinking in terms of romance. I was just thinking about sex. The last time I had sex was December. But romance...? I don't know if I've had that since I was a teenager. If then."

Sophia rolled over onto her stomach. "You've never been in love?"

"It's not easy when you're on the road all the time."

"I suppose that's true. But it's still very sad."

Chaplin made a noncommittal move with her head. "I

suppose. It's not really something I was looking for." She looked at Sophia. "Oh. I don't mean to imply this wasn't~"

Sophia laughed. "Don't worry yourself about me. I know what this is." She bowed her head and kissed the swell of Chaplin's breast. "It was very lovely. And I'll definitely do it again as much as you're willing. But I'm not expecting anything more from you."

Chaplin relaxed. "It's not about you..."

"I know," Sophia said softly. "But thank you for saying it anyway." She pinched the cigarette from Chaplin's fingers, took a drag. "What are you going to tell Edith about all of this? Will we have to sneak around once she's home? Just to be clear, that's not going to be a downside if your answer is yes. Sneaking around sounds like it could be a lot of fun."

Chaplin smiled. "I don't know yet." She looked toward the window, which faced the street. If Tinker had come home at any point, the headlights would have swept across the front of the house to announce her arrival. It irked her, not knowing what had happened in Santa Fe. "Whatever I decide, I don't have to say anything until at least the morning. So I'm not going to waste this glowing, feathery feeling I have worrying."

"We could always enhance that feeling," Sophia said.

"Oh?"

Sophia arched an eyebrow. She stretched across Chaplin's body to put the cigarette in the ashtray, her bare breasts brushing over Chaplin's in the process. She pulled halfway back so their faces were lined up and bent down to brush her lips across Chaplin's cheeks, then her mouth. They kissed as Sophia repositioned herself so she was straddling Chaplin's right leg.

"What's your plan here, Miss Ellis?"

"Feel my thigh against you?"

"Oh, I definitely am aware of that, yes."

Sophia grinned and put a hand on Chaplin's hip. She raised the other hand, gripped the headboard, and braced her knees against the mattress. She rolled her hips forward. Chaplin's eyes widened and she gasped, moving her hands so her fingers crossed in the small of Sophia's back. She bit her bottom lip and helped guide Sophia's movements, holding eye contact, rising to meet every thrust.

"It's not forever," Sophia said. "It doesn't have to be. It just has to be... right now. Here. This."

Chaplin smiled and nodded.

"That's enough for me."

Chaplin tightened her grip and held Sophia in place, leaning up to kiss her lips.

It was enough for her, too. She relaxed her arms and let Sophia go back to what she'd been doing. If this was the only night they had, then she was going to appreciate every single second of it.

CHAPTER ELEVEN

SANTA FE

Thursday July 12, 1945

Tinker should have expected Riggs would have a flair for the dramatic, even when it came to holding someone hostage.

After Riggs confirmed they'd caught the right person, he'd told Vernon to "take her back to the room," which turned out to be a hotel in the middle of town. She could see the rage mixing with excitement in his eyes as he gave the order. She could tell he was irritated he had to do the revival and couldn't deal with her immediately. But revenge, as sweet as it might be, paled in comparison to his potential earnings. If he was patient, he could have his cake and eat it, too.

And so Vernon had taken her to the hotel. He'd kept her silent on their way through the lobby and upstairs by pressing the tip of a knife against her kidney.

"Your boss would be pissed if you ruined his victory," she said as she was forced up the stairs.

"I figure I could keep you alive until he showed up to finish the job." Vernon jabbed her. She hissed, worried he might have broken the skin with the poke. "He'd be a lot more upset if I let you get away. So keep on walking."

That was how she ended up sitting on the tile floor of a hotel bathroom with her left wrist chained to the radiator. She had to keep her arm elevated so it wouldn't rest on the hot pipes, and her shoulder already ached something fierce.

The only advantage she had, other than her right hand being free, was that she didn't think they would kill her. Riggs definitely would want to keep her alive until he also had Chaplin. That was the one bright spot about the whole mess. He would assume she was somewhere in Santa Fe. There was no reason for him to think she'd driven sixty miles away from her partner to gather information on the revival. She just had to hope Chaplin was smart enough to not come looking for her.

Vernon had been tasked with watching her. She didn't remember him from the previous run-ins with Riggs, so she assumed he was a relatively new addition to the team. He was probably eager to prove his worth to the Reverend. Green and eager was a dangerous combination. He might go overboard, he might try too hard, he might decide he needed to make an example out of her.

There were a hundred ways the next few hours could go very wrong. But there were a handful of ways it could go perfectly for her. Green and eager could also be dangerous for Vernon. It made him goal-oriented. It would make him stupid in ways that she might be able to manipulate. She just had to be very careful how she approached him and what she said.

In other words, she needed to take her time. And that was something she didn't have.

Vernon had pulled a chair from somewhere in the room and placed it in front of the bathroom door. It gave him a line of sight to her, and also blocked her from having a direct line to the hotel room door, so she couldn't escape without going through him.

"This is a pretty swell assignment for you," Tinker said.

He stared.

"I'm just saying that in case you didn't know. I don't remember seeing you last year when we caused Riggs so much trouble, so he may not have clued you into the whole story."

"Rev has enemies," Vernon said. "You're one of 'em. That's all I need to know."

She narrowed her eyes. "It's kind of odd for a reverend to have enemies. Don't you think?"

"He's not your ordinary reverend."

"You got that right." Tinker rested her head against the wall. She couldn't help thinking about what Riggs had said in the car. Her father. She would have dismissed it as a pathetic attempt to intimidate her, but he'd said her real name. There was only one way he could know that, and it was he was telling the truth. She had to accept it was a real threat.

"So Riggs found my father, huh? Shame. I had been assuming he was long dead."

"Nope. Alive and kicking in Galveston. Rev is probably sending him a telegram as we speak."

Tinker tried not to let her fear show. "Might be nice to see the old man again."

Vernon chuckled. "Yeah, not the way he talked about you."

"It's insanely good luck, though. Imagine, running into the father of the person who destroyed your business. The chances of that!"

"Ain't no luck or chance," Vernon said, taking her bait. "Rev wasn't going to let y'all get away with what you did. So he went all around asking about you. Describing y'all. People remember an old lady running around with a ginger."

"Hey!" Tinker twisted to look at him. "I'm fifty. That's not old. And she's not ginger, she's strawberry blonde."

Vernon ignored her. "Pretty soon word got around. Your daddy heard we were looking at came to find us."

"Oh! So he didn't even do anything. My father came to him. That makes more sense." She laughed. "I was having a heck of a time picturing Riggs being effective at all."

"He found you didn't he?"

"No!" Tinker laughed. "I fell into his lap, too! Because I was stupid and parked my truck on the street where any idiot could drive by and see it. He has good eyesight, I suppose. I'll grant him that. And he's the luckiest son of a bitch on the planet. Or I'm the unluckiest. One or the other."

Vernon stood up and walked into the bathroom. "Stop saying that. He prayed to find you and–"

"Oh God," Tinker said, laughing harder. "Don't tell me you actually believe in his hogwash. He's a con man. He's lying to all these people. Do you honestly think he has healing powers?"

"I've seen it with my own eyes!"

Tinker looked at him with real sympathy. "Oh. Oh, no. Well, now I feel insulted. I thought he left you here by yourself because he trusted you. But he just wanted you out of the way. If he doesn't even trust you with the main lie of his whole organization..." She shook her head. "You don't even get to weed through the audience to find marks, do you?"

Vernon loomed over her. "Listen—"

The one step he had taken to wag a finger in her face was all she needed. She kicked him hard just above the right knee. His leg crumpled under his weight and he went down hard, falling forward with his hands outstretched to break his fall. He grabbed the radiator and the sizzling sound was sickening, but Tinker didn't waste much time feeling pity for him as he fell on top of her.

She wrapped her legs around him and used her weight to flip him over onto the floor. The move made her shackled arm press against the radiator and she clenched her teeth against the stab of burning pain that resulted. *Only fair, since I burned him,* she thought.

Vernon screamed, too busy staring at his burned hands to fight her off as she rooted around in his pockets for the handcuff key. She found it quickly, then twisted and unlocked herself.

"Stop, get... g-get back..." Vernon was panting on the floor, face beet-red and beaded with sweat. "S-stop..."

Tinker was breathless. The burn on her arm was killing her, and she could only imagine how Vernon felt. It probably wouldn't blister but it had to be agonizing.

"Bit of advice?" she said. "Next time, find a boss worthy of getting the top layer of skin burned off your hands. Riggs doesn't give a shit about you, and he doesn't deserve that kind of loyalty."

She left before he could recover from the pain and shock. She didn't know if it was safe to go back to her truck, if it was even still there. They might have just lost everything because she had gotten lazy and distracted. But there was nowhere else for her to go, so that was where she headed.

The truck wasn't far from the hotel. She kept to the side roads and alleys whenever possible. The neighborhood seemed mostly abandoned. Hopefully everyone was at the revival and she could make a clean getaway. She assumed at least Riggs and his cronies would be occupied there. They wouldn't have any reason to stake out the truck since they most likely thought Vernon had her locked up tight at the hotel.

Still, when she arrived and saw the truck was still there, she held back. She stayed in the alley and watched the street for any signs of surveillance. She watched the truck to see if the chassis was weighed down, indicating a body waiting in the front seat for her again. Both doors seemed tightly shut. The tarp over the bed flapped in the breeze and she couldn't see any telltale signs of anyone hiding underneath.

She waited ten minutes before she dared approach. This time she came up on the truck from behind, on the passenger side, peeking through the back window before accepting the truck really was vacant. She fished the keys from her pocket and, taking one last look to make sure the street was still deserted, she got behind the wheel and drove away from the curb.

A car passed her at the city limits, which triggered a thought so terrifying that she had to pull off on the shoulder to contemplate it. She had to think about what she knew about Riggs, Osker, and Vernon and how they might approach the situation.

Riggs had left a man waiting at her truck. He couldn't have known when or if she would come back, so Osker had obviously been willing to wait as long as possible. If he agreed to that, then it proved he was a patient man. He wouldn't care about his discomfort if it paid off in the end.

And Vernon? The man was obviously an imbecile. She hadn't even had to be particularly clever to trick him. Riggs and Osker would both have chosen to guard her themselves before they entrusted someone like him with the assignment.

Unless the assignment wasn't to keep her in the hotel room.

Leaving her with Vernon only made sense if she was supposed to get away.

She looked in the rearview mirror, then twisted to look out the back window as if it might show her a different picture.

Riggs might have been a lucky piece of trash, but he could be clever. He was a successful con man, after all, and he'd been in the process of following the breadcrumbs to find them when her father saved him the trouble. Wasn't that just another sign of cleverness? Letting someone else do the hard work for you?

For instance, why expend time and resources searching the entire city for where Chaplin was hiding when he could just have Tinker lead him there?

She settled back against the seat and put her hands on the steering wheel.

There were no vehicles behind her, at least none that she'd seen. They might have pulled over as soon as she did. She could see a few parked cars on the mile or see stretch she had just driven. Had they been there when she passed? She honestly couldn't tell for sure. And maybe her tail had kept driving so as not to raise suspicions. The car that passed her could have pulled off up ahead, around the corner, and might be waiting for her at this very moment.

The only thing she knew for certain was that she couldn't go back to Sophia's house until she was absolutely certain she wasn't being followed. Another mile or so, and she'd be in the open desert, and it would be a lot more noticeable if someone was trying to keep a tail on her.

She checked the road one more time before she started driving again. She kept an eye on the rearview and side mirrors as much as she dared. No one seemed to pull out behind her, but that was no guarantee. She'd already made one mistake by walking directly into Riggs' grasp. She wasn't going to compound it by being lazy now.

She pressed her foot down on the accelerator, heading off down the long ribbon of road into the desert.

INTERLUDE

MAYPEARL, TEXAS
Monday April 22, 1912

Tinker's first memory of her father was from her first night living with him. Her bedroom was a closet in a rowhouse she'd never seen before. She was given a cushion from an old couch and a threadbare sheet she could use as a blanket. Then her father said he'd see her in the morning and closed the door on her. It took her three days to realize she was there because her mother had died. No one ever confirmed it. There was no funeral, and she never saw a body, but she knew it was the only explanation that made sense. Her mother would never have left her in that place unless she was gone.

It was almost two months before her father figured out what to do with her. He discovered people were soft for a little girl with bright blue eyes a dirty face, and started sending her out to "earn her dinner." She was also a great distraction when he had bigger jobs that needed to be done. Send out the kid, let everyone focus on her, and he could slip around emptying pockets and purses without being noticed.

One night Tinker came out of her room in search of water. Her father was sitting around the table with some of his friends playing a card game. One of them spotted her and swore. "Damn, I didn't know you had a kid."

Her father had twisted to look at her, then turned his back on her. "Yeah. It's useful sometimes."

He started training her to help out more after that. He taught her how to pick a pocket, spot marks, the right way to fall without hurting herself. Her hands were smaller than his, and people were much less suspicious of a little girl getting close to them than a full-grown man. If she was caught with her hand in someone's purse, she could just say she was looking for candy or thought the woman was her mother. People believed any lie that came out of a child's mouth. She became his secret weapon, and suddenly business was booming.

She learned to love the games they played. She was only vaguely aware how their stories and tricks connected to the food on their table, or why sometimes she got dragged out of bed and forced to pack in the middle of the night. She didn't understand why her father would pull the brim of his hat down whenever he saw a policeman, but she started doing the same.

Things were perfect until she was twelve or thirteen. Suddenly she was taller. Her arms were weirdly long, and sometimes she tripped over her own feet. The people who had once called her adorable would look at her sideways. They never smiled at her anymore. She started getting caught more just because people were paying more attention. Her old lies didn't work once she started to look like a teenager.

One night she overheard her father talking about her with his gambling buddies. "Damned useless to me now," he said. "I might as well be out there with a dog."

"She could always take after her mama," one of his friends suggested. "You'd bring in some good money that way."

"She's still a damn kid, you cretin," her father said. "I ain't interested in dealing with the kind of people that would bring around."

"Okay, okay, but maybe in a few years."

"Maybe in a few years," her father agreed. "But that doesn't put food on the table tonight."

Tinker was old enough, and street smart enough, to know her father's resolve wouldn't last a few years. If they had enough busts, if they went enough nights hungry, he would slip. Once or twice wouldn't be so bad. It would be fine if he only invited people he knew. She had no doubts that in less than a year, he would start introducing her to some of his friends with instructions to "treat them well."

She started planning her escape that night. It took her two weeks to figure out how to get his stash, and another month to get up the courage to actually clean him out and leave. She waited until the carnival was in town. They traveled by train and, as far as she knew, it was the fastest and easiest way to put distance between her and her father. She found out the schedule and arranged to be aboard the train when it pulled out.

A storm blew in the night she left, slipping out the window as the sky sparked with lightning as if trying to ruin her plan. The rain fell like waves of water, slapping her in the face as she ran down the middle of the road, arms pumping as she squinted through the downpour, desperate to get to safety. She didn't know if the carnival would be better, but at least she would have a better chance to become a real person there.

The carnies were still loading everything up when she arrived. She didn't say anything to anybody. She found someone who was carrying a crate too big for one person and positioned herself at the opposite side. She took its weight and started walking. The other person craned his neck to see why his load had suddenly become lighter. Tinker had ignored the look and focused on where they were going. After a moment, the man shrugged and looked away from her and continued walking.

She continued helping through the night, always worried that a sweep of headlights would announce the arrival of her father to drag her home. When she heard the all-clear, she climbed into one of the cars and found a space large enough for her to squeeze into.

When she was discovered at their next stop, she was dragged out and marched to the carnival owner. His office took up most of an entire train car and was decorated like the penthouse of a grand hotel. He was smoking a cigar despite the early hour, squinting at her through the smoke as she told her story. A woman in a black-and-gold robe, a fortune teller named Greta, sat on the divan reading a newspaper. She seemed completely indifferent to everything happening a few feet away from her until Tinker's voice gave out. She bowed her head and sniffled, hoping against hope that it would be too much trouble to send her back home.

Greta folded the newspaper in her lap and looked at the owner like a disappointed teacher. "Don't pretend you have to think about it, Martin."

Tinker and Martin both looked at Greta. She waved her manicured fingers in Tinker's direction.

"A girl this age doesn't wind up on a carnival train in the middle of the night because she's bored. No one ends up like this unless she's running from something." She looked at Tinker, holding eye contact. "Something bad, I'll bet."

Tinker sniffled and nodded.

"You can't send her back to that," Greta said.

"She stays, you're responsible for her."

Greta shrugged and put the newspaper aside. She unfolded herself from the couch and held out a hand to Tinker.

"Come on, sweetheart. Let's go get you some breakfast and we can talk about what you have to offer us."

Tinker took Greta's hand, still sniffling. She was grateful for the rescue, certain that the skills her father had given her would be more than enough to earn her place among these outcasts.

For the first time since she overheard her father call her useless, she allowed herself to relax.

CHAPTER TWELVE

ALBUQUERQUE
Friday July 13, 1945

Chaplin's first reaction to waking up in Sophia's arms was panic. She was worried Tinker had come home in the night and now there would be no chance of concealing what had happened. All it took was one glance down at Sophia's slumped face for all that worry to slip away. She was absolutely gorgeous, with her cheek flat against Chaplin's shoulder, her lips slack and parted as if she was in the middle of making an O sound. It didn't matter if Tinker was home, if they'd been caught. It would be worth it for waking up next to this sight.

So she remained right where she was, pinned under Sophia's left arm and leg. She didn't have to wait long before Sophia stirred. Her body stiffened slightly, her fingers pressed against Chaplin's side, and she turned her head to brush her lips over the pillow. She sat up and cracked one eye open, blinking until it focused on the face smiling back at her.

"Good morning," Chaplin said.

"Mm-hmm," Sophia said, rolling to one side. She pushed herself up to rest her shoulders against the headboard. "How much sleep did we actually get?"

Chaplin looked at the alarm clock. "I don't know. I didn't look at the time when we finally passed out. But it's a little after six o'clock now."

Sophia suddenly sat straight up, muttering a curse under her breath as she swung her legs around onto the floor. She moved so quickly that she was almost to the door before Chaplin could get a word out.

"What's wrong?"

"I have..." Sophia stopped and rested her hand on the doorknob. She half-turned so Chaplin could see her profile. She looked confused. "I-I have to be at work at seven-thirty."

Chaplin nodded. "Okay. It seems like you have plenty of time."

"Yeah." Sophia turned to look at her. "Yeah," she said again. "Plenty of time."

Chaplin pushed back the blanket and got out of bed. They were both naked, and she regretted that she didn't have the time to appreciate the sight of Sophia's body in the sunlight.

"What did you think you had to do?"

Sophia pushed her hands through her hair. She walked back to the bed and sat down on the edge of the mattress.

"Before my mother... When I was still taking care of her, I had to take care of her before I went to work. Get her up, make sure she was dressed and her hair was done, make her breakfast. It was a whole production. Sometimes it took two hours just to get everything done. I had to wake up before dawn to make sure she was situated and I could get to work on time."

Chaplin approached carefully, as if Sophia was a wild animal that could be spooked. "So maybe I *did* see you in the kitchen the other night."

"What?" Sophia looked at her. "No. No, I was confused just now, that's all."

Chaplin knelt in front of Sophia and took her hands. "You spent a long time putting your mother's needs before yours. Maybe your body still hasn't gotten the message that it's okay to rest. So it gets you up out of bed and sends you through the motions even though it doesn't need to."

Sophia stared at her. "That's not something that... happens to people."

"Are you sure you've let your mother go? Do you completely accept that she doesn't need you anymore?"

"She..." Tears filled Sophia's eyes. "I don't know. I think so?"

Chaplin kissed Sophia's knuckles. "You just jumped out of bed like you'd been pricked in the ass by a needle. You thought you were running behind. Maybe muscle memory has been making you do the same thing every night. Do you feel exhausted in the morning even though you go to bed early?"

"Well, sure, but who... who doesn't?"

"Plenty of people," Chaplin said. "How do you feel this morning?"

Sophia smiled, and a tear slid free. "After last night? Sore, and tired, and tingly."

Chaplin laughed. She squeezed Sophia's fingers. "I think the reason you didn't sleepwalk to the kitchen last night is because you were actually thinking of yourself for a change. I'm glad I could give that to you."

"I'm glad, too." Sophia's voice was soft. She tucked her bottom lip under her teeth and ran her eyes over Chaplin's face. "Goodness, but you're beautiful, Margaret Byrd."

Chaplin's smile wavered.

"What is it? What's wrong?"

"Nothing." Chaplin leaned in and kissed Sophia's lips. "Nothing's wrong, not this morning." She kissed Sophia again, and the gentle peck turned into something deeper, more passionate.

She put her hands on Sophia's shoulders to ease her down onto the mattress. Sophia allowed herself to be laid down, her eyes open in the kiss as she moved her hands to Chaplin's hips to help her climb up onto the mattress.

Chaplin settled on top of her. She didn't have to worry about names, or lies, or anything else except this moment and this morning. This was something which had to be savored before it slipped away. She intended to give it her full attention.

Everything else would work itself out later.

When they finally managed to get out of bed for good, Chaplin glanced out the window and stopped walking. Sophia pressed against her from behind and wrapped both arms around her waist. She nuzzled Chaplin's neck.

"What's wrong?"

"The truck isn't here."

Sophia looked out the window. "Maybe the business took longer than she expected and she decided to stay overnight. The road between here and Santa Fe can get really dark at night. It's scary."

"I know," Chaplin said. "But it's weird. And we... sort of had an argument before she left. It's not important what it was about, but it makes me more concerned than I would be otherwise."

Sophia let her go and moved to stand beside her. "Do you think something might have happened to her?"

"No," Chaplin said, not letting her think about the possibility. "No, I'm sure the argument actually explains where she is. Giving us both space to cool down."

"It's not about me, is it?" Sophia asked.

Chaplin looked at her. "Why would you think that?"

Sophia chuckled softly and shook her head. She turned and went into the kitchen. "Forget I said anything, it's nothing."

"What?"

"It's just that it wasn't really the age difference that made me realize you weren't sisters, that's all. Or the fact you two don't look anything alike. It was because at the first dinner we had together, you kept looking at me in a way that made me think you were interested. And Edith noticed. And she did *not* like it. I think she kind of hates me."

Chaplin shook her head. "No. No, she doesn't hate you... It's more complicated than that." She plucked at the hem of her shirt. "She has feelings for me. She has for a long time. At Christmas, we crossed the line. And I thought it would get it out of her system. I thought we could move on from it. Hell, I thought we *had* moved on. But now she's acting weird."

Sophia sighed. "Oh, dear. You don't know anything, do you."

"What?"

"You thought it would *end* how she felt about you? Darling, you gave her everything she wanted and now she knows exactly what she's missing out on. No wonder she's angry at you."

Chaplin grimaced. "It's not my fault she has those feelings for me."

"No, it isn't," Sophia said, her voice soft. "And it's not your fault that you don't feel the same. Love is fickle and unfair. All we can do is try to manage it and understand each other when things don't line up just right. I think you and Edith found a balance and then it got screwed up when you slept together. You were able to walk away and go back to normal. She wasn't."

"So what am I supposed to do?"

"Give her space." Sophia shrugged. "You might not get back to where you were before, but you might be able to find another good place. Like I said, you had balance. But now there's an added weight and you need to adjust before you topple over."

She turned away and went into the icebox to get the things she needed to start breakfast. Chaplin looked out the window again, at the empty driveway that signified Tinker's absence. Maybe there was a chance they could find a new balance, a new way to stand they could find a new normal.

Or maybe the added weight was what would finally knock them to the ground. Maybe they were just flailing around, seconds away from falling flat on their faces.

INTERLUDE

COLUMBUS, OHIO
Thursday July 17, 1941

Earlier that night, the Cleveland Indians - specifically pitchers Al Smith and Jim Bagby, Jr. - had broken DiMaggio's hitting streak. Even though the Yankees went on to win the game, it was considered a victory due to taking "Joltin' Joe" down a peg. The bar was full of Indians fans celebrating the honor, so Tinker and Chaplin made it a point to be present to take advantage of a large group of drunk people in a confined space. They picked pockets, they accepted drinks that men bought for "the pretty ladies at the end of the bar," and they played whatever hustles they could think of.

"Do you have a coin in your pocket?" Chaplin asked a man next to her.

He smiled and turned to face her fully. "I sure do, sweetie. Want me to buy you a drink with it?"

"If things work out, you'll buy me lots of drinks. Want to see a magic trick?"

"Sure, darling." His friend also turned and was paying attention now.

Chaplin folded her arms on the bar. "Take out the coin and

put it under that coaster. Don't let me see it. I bet you five bucks I can tell you the date."

The man raised an eyebrow. He dug in his pocket, produced a coin, and glanced at the face to see the date. Then he placed it under the coaster. He placed his hand on top of the coaster and looked at her.

"Okay. What's the date?"

"July 17, 1941," she said.

The man stared at her for a second, lips parted in confusion. Then his friend guffawed and slapped him on the shoulder.

"She never said *the date on the coin*," the friend laughed. "Oh, that's good. I'm going to remember that one!" He slapped his friend on the shoulder again, harder this time. "Go on, pay the woman! She earned it!"

The mark's smile was forced, but he placed the money on the bar. Chaplin bought him a drink with her winnings to ease any hurt feelings he might have otherwise let brew.

When she had fleeced all the sheep at the bar, she weaved through the crowd to see what Tinker had gotten up to. She was at a table near the back betting someone she could drink three full beers and three shots before anyone else at the table.

"You can't touch any of my glasses, and I can't touch any of yours, just to make sure there's no funny business," Tinker was saying to her marks.

Chaplin smiled, envisioning how the game would play out. Tinker would drink her first beer in a single go, then place her empty glass upside down over one of her opponent's shots. Since the rules clearly stated he wasn't allowed to touch her glasses, and she hadn't broken the rule by touching his, she could tackle the rest of her drinks at her leisure. The loser would have to pay for all twelve drinks. It was a brutal and expensive game, but the fool accepted her terms and motioned for the bartender.

Tinker caught Chaplin's eye and gave her a wink. Chaplin winked back and moved on, trying to see if there were more victims waiting to give her their cash.

Instead, she found a brunette seated at the far end of the bar nursing a beer. She was using a toothpick to draw designs on the watermarks left on the bar. When she looked up at Chaplin, her green eyes sparkled and danced. She smiled and folded her fingers around the toothpick, turning on her stool in what could only be an invitation to approach.

Chaplin slipped into the open space next to the mystery woman, grateful that the crowd let her get much closer than she otherwise would've gotten away with.

"Well, hello there," Chaplin said.

"Hi. Are you going to con me into buying you a drink?"

Chaplin grinned. "So you've been watching me."

"You're hard to miss, darling."

Chaplin's grin widened. "I've had a pretty good night. Maybe I'll share the wealth." She held out her hand. "My name is Penny."

"Angela."

The woman took Chaplin's hand, and Penny brought it to her lips to kiss the knuckles. She looked up into Angela's eyes. The kiss was a question, and Angela's eyes had the answer. Chaplin straightened and rolled her shoulders back, lips curling into a knowing smile. Angela returned the smile and tilted her head to one side. The pink tip of her tongue brushed over her bottom lip. Easy to miss unless someone was looking for it.

"Actually, I've had a lot to drink," Chaplin said. "All this smoke and all these people. How about we get some fresh air?"

"I could use a breather," Angela said. "Lead the way."

Five minutes later, Chaplin was on top of Angela in the seat of their truck. Her right hand was under Angela's dress, her left clumsily working the buttons of the bodice. They were kissing, Angela's thigh was pressing between Chaplin's legs, and clothes had just become far too complicated to be attempting one-handed.

The light coming in through the driver's side window changed. Chaplin lifted her head and saw Tinker's unmistakable silhouette looking down at them. She had been reaching for the door handle and recoiled when she saw what was happening in the seat. Their eyes locked, and there was a strange look in her eyes that Chaplin couldn't quite identify. They held each other's gaze for a heartbeat before Tinker's mask slipped back into place. She dropped her hand, turned, and quickly walked away.

"Shit," Angela said, squirming onto her side. Her entire body had gone rigid, and Chaplin knew their tryst had just come to an undeniable end. "If that woman tells my husband~"

"She's not going to tell anyone." Chaplin lifted off of Angela and moved to the passenger side of the seat. "Just relax. It's fine. It's all going to be fine."

Angela leapt from the truck on the driver's side. She quickly vanished into the darkness. Chaplin buttoned up her blouse and went in pursuit of her partner. He was fairly sure Tinker wouldn't have a problem with her proclivities, but it wasn't something they'd ever talked about.

Tinker was on the sidewalk outside the bar. Her arms were crossed over her chest and her head was down, staring at her feet as she paced in a tight circle.

"Hey. Um. About that..."

"Don't."

Chaplin was still tucking her shirt into her slacks. "No, I think we should talk about it."

Tinker looked up and met her eyes. "I don't think we do."

"I need to know it's not an issue. The fact that I'm..." She cut her eyes toward the front window of the bar. "That I'm like that. It's bound to come up if we're going to be traveling together. If you have a problem with it~"

"I'm like that, too," Tinker said sharply. "I'm... I don't have a problem with that, because I'm the same. Okay?"

Chaplin raised her eyebrows. "Oh." She laughed. "Okay. I just figured by your reaction... There was this look on your face when you saw us that was almost like disgust or~" The pieces clicked in her head. "Oh...! Were you jealous? You probably had your eye on her first and I just swooped in and snapped her up."

"What? No. I didn't even see who it was. I just saw the... hair and the lace slip under her dress."

Chaplin furrowed her brow. Jealousy seemed like the absolute correct emotion for what she'd seen in Tinker's unguarded reaction. It was an unmistakable mixture of sadness, anger, betrayal. She hadn't known Tinker long, but she'd seen a whole range of feelings on the woman's face through various cons. Jealousy was the only one that made sense. But if she'd hadn't seen Angela, then~

Chaplin looked at Tinker, who was making a point not to look at her.

"Oh."

Tinker still didn't look at her. "What." She said the word without inflection or emotion, barely any volume. Her arms tightened around herself as if bracing for a blow.

"Nothing," Chaplin said softly. "I j-just... I guess I was wrong."

She scratched the side of her neck. Somehow realizing this about her friend seemed much more intimate than what Tinker had just caught her doing. Her face burned and she hoped the street was too dark for Tinker to notice.

"Maybe we should go back in the bar. There are still a few sheep to shear in there."

"Actually, I'm pretty beat. I was going to catch a nap in the truck until you were finished."

Chaplin nodded. "Oh. Okay..."

Tinker turned and started to walk back to the truck. "Take your time."

"Hey, Tinker," Chaplin said.

Tinker looked back at her.

Chaplin didn't know what to say. "Have a good nap."

Tinker smiled. "Thanks, Penny."

She walked away, and Chaplin remained in front of the bar. She didn't feel like going back inside. On a normal night, she would have taken a nap next to Tinker in the truck and then they would head out on the road when they were rested. But that didn't seem like an option tonight. Somehow it seemed like the best thing to do for their partnership would be to just give her some space.

She breathed in deep, let it out slowly, and went into the bar to drown her emotions.

CHAPTER THIRTEEN

FIFTY MILES SOUTHWEST OF ALBUQUERQUE
Friday July 13, 1945

Tinker didn't sleep at all that night. She drove, occasionally pushing up the cuff of her sleeve to scratch at the burn from the radiator. Damn thing didn't hurt so much as sting, and the sting was a pain in the butt. It was dark by the time she got back to Albuquerque. She stopped at a filling station just long enough to top off on gas and get supplies, but she made sure she did it far away from Sophia Ellis and the guesthouse to minimize the risk of Chaplin wandering out into view.

When she pulled back onto the road with a full tank of gas, a forest-green Nash 600 pulled out from a nearby lot and fell in behind her. She put on a little speed. It matched her. She slowed down, and it matched that as well. His headlights were on, which meant he either assumed she'd made him or didn't care if she noticed. She felt an uncomfortable combination of vindication, anger, and fear that she had been right. She tightened her grip on the steering wheel until her fingers hurt, until she was positive she was leaving indentations in the leather that would never come out.

She let herself feel the rage for a few miles before she started thinking strategically. She kept one hand on the steering wheel as she reached for the glove compartment and retrieved the map. It took some effort to get it open without veering all over the road but she eventually managed it. She held the map on the steering wheel by pinning the top edge with her thumb, using her free hand to aim a flashlight at the paper. The truck wobbled but stayed true, just barely. She alternated between watching the road and trying to figure out where the hell she was going to run.

The map showed her a smattering of small towns in the foothills south of Albuquerque. It looked confusing enough that it would easy to either get lost there or at the very least confuse whoever was in the Nash. She kept driving until she was almost fifty miles from the city limits, deeming that a safe distance, before she pulled off the highway. She took the first turn she came to, knowing she wouldn't lose the Nash that easily. The land was too flat and she was kicking up a plume of dust.

Sure enough, a few minutes after she left the main road, the Nash followed. The road revealed by the sweep of her headlights was a cracked ribbon cutting through a seemingly endless sea of scrub that stretched out to either side. Hills marked the horizon on either side, like walls rising on the edges of the world. Fortunately all the wide open space and wide expanse of sky saved her from feeling claustrophobic.

Ideally, she would have found a bolt hole, somewhere she could duck into and hide in a moment just like this. And it was their own damned faults for it. They'd gotten lazy. They saw the revival sign and just acted on instinct. She cursed herself for not doing the bare minimum of prep for this job. There was no excuse for it. They'd had the time. Instead they had wasted their head start by scamming a grocery store and getting cozy with a random citizen.

There was nothing to be done about it now. The only thing she could do was make sure they learned from it so they were never caught so off-guard in the future.

It seemed as if most of the buildings she passed were churches, schools, or private property with long driveways blocked by gates. None of them would work for what she needed. She eyed her gas gauge and checked her rearview. The Nash was still behind her, still keeping his distance. He had to realize this was a wild goose chase. There was no chance she hadn't seen him, and even less of a chance that she would be stupid enough to go back to Chaplin with that information.

Tinker checked her gas levels again. There was plenty to get her back to Albuquerque even with all this wandering around in the foothills. But that was with the fill-up, which the Nash didn't have the chance to get. If he had left Santa Fe with a full tank, then there was a chance he was driving on fumes now. She had forced him to drive to his limits and he still hadn't slowed down, hesitated, or given up. He was willing to strand himself out here for Riggs.

"All right," she muttered under his breath. "He wants to sacrifice himself for the Rev? Let's give the man what he wants."

She pulled onto a side road and drive west. The map showed a meager branch of the Rio Grande cut north-to-south nearby. She had to take a few private roads to get close, and even then she eventually reached a point where she couldn't get any closer unless she was on foot. She parked in the middle of the road and got out of the truck. She kept her flashlight and the keys and waited, looking back the way she'd come.

Eventually the Nash appeared, a dark and rumbling silhouette at the intersection she had just taken. Tinker turned on the flashlight and lifted it above her head. She aimed the beam at their car and waved it in an arc, left-right, left-right, just to make sure they saw her.

Then she ran.

She didn't stop until she reached the water. This part of the river was probably weak and narrow enough that she could cross, but she had no intention of abandoning their truck or stranding herself out here. She stopped on stood in the mud to look back the way she had come.

The Nash occupants were following her at a leisurely pace. She thought she could see two silhouettes behind the flashlight beam, but there could have been more waiting in the car or at her truck. It all came down to how many people Riggs was willing to risk on this assignment, and two seemed like a good amount. Four was basically his entire inner circle.

"You're an elusive woman, Missus Driscoll," a familiar voice called.

She curved a hand above her eyes, as if the flashlight was blinding her. "Osker? Is that you? Well, imagine running into you all the way out here. And who is that with you? Did you bring Vernon? Or has he served his purpose in this little game you set up?"

The men stopped. "I have to admit, neither of us realized what you were doing until we got outside Albuquerque back there,"

Osker said. "We knew you'd twigged to us early on, but we figured you would still head back to your buddy to brainstorm the next step."

"So all this time, you still think I'm an idiot. That's wonderful." It actually was a relief. It was so much easier to trick people who underestimated her intelligence. But it was still annoying that they hadn't figured out she was smarter than them yet.

"We don't need to make this hard, Missus Driscoll. The Rev doesn't like resorting to violent means. He just wants to make sure you and the other Byrd girl keep your noses out of his business. He's trying to rebuild after what you girls did to him. It will go a lot easier if he's not looking over his shoulder all the damn time wondering if you're about to pop up and screw everything up again."

Tinker shrugged. "So we all just ignore each other from here on? I can go along with that."

Osker laughed. "I wish we could take your word for that, Missus Driscoll. But honestly, would *you* believe *us* if we said we were just going to let bygones be bygones? After everything we've been through, and all we know about each other, there's no trust here. We can't just wave a white flag and go on our merry ways. Today proved that. We're bound to keep bumping into each other as long as we're both on the same road. So the Rev needs to make sure you're... somewhere else."

"By handing me over to my father." Tinker was glad they couldn't see the look of disgust on her face. "I was hoping I could just wait him out. Have you seen him? He's got to be on his last gasp, right? The man was the live fast and die young sort, you know."

"I've spoken with him, yes. People have a habit of staying alive when they have a purpose. You gave him a very strong purpose, Missus Driscoll."

"You can just call me Tinker."

"Why would I do that when I know it isn't your name?" Osker and the other man were moving closer now. "We hoped that we could control this situation. We wanted to get you and the other woman at the same time so you would have no choice but to cooperate. But now we can see we'll need you to be involved. So here is what will happen. You'll take us to wherever it is you have your little friend hiding out. Then the four of us go back to Santa

Fe, and we hold tight until Reverend Riggs is finished with the revival. By that time, either your daddy will have made his way to town to retrieve you, or you'll come along with us to our next stop."

Tinker said, "My father doesn't give a damn about Chaplin. What's going to happen to her in this little plan of yours?"

"I don't think you're in a position to worry about her, Missus Dr~ Tinker."

She walked toward them, further closing the distance. "No, I think *you're* the one in a bad position, Osker. Because you drove that little Nash all the way from Santa Fe and you never stopped for fuel. You couldn't have, because you couldn't run the risk I'd give you the shake. So when we go back to our vehicles, I'll go along my merry way, but you two can only follow for a handful more miles before you end up by the side of the road."

Silence from the other side of the beam.

"So here's the deal for *you*," she said. "We go back. I siphon off just enough gas from my truck to get you back to a station in Albuquerque. Then you go back to Santa Fe by yourselves and tell Riggs that I gave you the slip."

"And we just let you go?" Osker said.

"The other option is you two just start walking. It doesn't feel too bad right now but once the sun comes up, you're going to have a rough time of it."

"The other option is that we take your truck." That was the other man, who had been silent up to this point. Tinker didn't recognize his voice.

"Well, you're certainly welcome to try that. But I'm going to make you fight for it. And I have a feeling whatever deal you struck with my father includes the fact that I remained unharmed. If I show up battered and bloodied, your precious Rev won't be too happy."

They were silent again.

She clucked her tongue. "Well, come on, gentlemen. The night is rolling on toward dawn. Shall we make an accord now or do you want to beat me up and steal my truck?"

Osker's flashlight lowered to aim at the ground. "The way I see it, we don't have much of a choice. We'll take your offer. But this won't be the last you hear from us, *Missus Driscoll*. The country is nowhere near as big as it seems, as we've discovered today. Our paths are bound to cross again and again."

"Sounds tiring," Tinker said. "You might want to consider

cutting your losses and calling it quits now while you're sort of ahead."

Osker sighed. "I could say the same to you."

"Right." Tinker gestured with her flashlight. "Lead the way, gentlemen."

They walked back to the road with Tinker trailing behind them, keeping an eye on both silhouettes to make sure neither of them tried anything. She shined her light at the unknown man's head and discovered he was blond. He twisted to look back at her and blocked the light from hitting his face by raising his hand. She could see a beard slightly darker than his hair and a low brow that shadowed his eyes. She'd seen him at Riggs' past revivals but had never caught his name.

"Hey, cut that out," he said.

"Just wanted to get a peek at you."

When they got back to the vehicles, Tinker let them fill a quarter of a metal can with gas from her tank. She let them drive off first to make sure they wouldn't just turn their headlights off and follow her when she drove away.

As soon as their taillights were no longer visible, she got back into her truck and checked the gauge. She had enough to get her back to Albuquerque, easy. The problem was that if Osker and Sandy Beard decided to hang around town, spend the night in a motel or get something to eat, she couldn't risk them spotting the truck. It wouldn't be safe for her to be back in Albuquerque for twelve hours at least, maybe even a full day.

She sat behind the wheel with the engine off as she considered her options. She couldn't go back to Sophia's house until she was sure Osker had passed through and gone back to Santa Fe. The closest town of any size was Hot Springs, over a hundred miles south of where she was currently sitting. She might be able to get there on her current fuel, but it would be tight. She would much rather find a place to lie low nearby so she didn't have to waste any more time on the road.

She unfolded the map again and used the flashlight to examine the area. She was looking for small towns, but places that might be big enough to support a service station. Maybe a diner or a motel where she could kick her feet up for a while to wait out the Rev's goons.

Wherever she ended up, it needed to be somewhere indoors in the shade. She'd bluffed Osker and Sandy Beard about a lot, but there was one thing she knew for sure...

It was going to be a scorcher.

INTERLUDE

MARIETTA, GEORGIA
Wednesday January 7, 1925
Tinker was going to be a millionaire.

She wasn't anywhere close yet, not even really in the ballpark, but she could see the day coming down the road. If they kept having months like they'd been having, if the money kept rolling in the way it had been, it was only a matter of time before they had more than she'd even know what to do with. They could buy a car each. They could buy their own house, one for each of them. Hell, at this rate, they might even be able to find legitimate jobs. Anything would be possible with more money than God.

And it had been so easy. Lafitte had explained the scam when she showed Tinker the office they'd be using. Tinker had been furious that she'd used so much of the money from their nest egg to rent the dusty, echoey cave in a shabby building on a dead-end street.

"We need a base of operations for this game," Lafitte had explained. "We need a place for our supplies, our merchandise, and a mailing address to legitimize us just enough to make the lie work."

"What's the lie?" Tinker crossed her arms over her chest, ready to argue.

Lafitte grinned. "We're going to solve a problem that men all around the world have suffered but not one will ever admit to experiencing."

Tinker shrugged, at a loss.

Lafitte held up her forefinger as if she was pointing to her right. Then she let the finger droop and she flicked it a few times.

"I'm talking about men experiencing... stifficulty."

"That's not really an area I have a lot of expertise in."

"Me neither," Lafitte said. "But that's not the point. We're not going to cure anything. We're just going to sell them the idea of a cure. Some kind of pill, a medicinal herb that's really just dried-out orange peels, water with food coloring added. It doesn't matter what the delivery method is. It's not going to work. We can make it for ten cents, sell it for ten bucks."

Tinker said, "And when it doesn't work?"

Lafitte laughed. "That's the beauty of it, my dear. Some of them? It *will* work. Either they'll believe in the medication enough that it will work, or they'll just happen to improve at the same time they start taking it. Either way, they'll assume the medicine did the trick. Or it won't work, but they'll be too embarrassed to cause a fuss by admitting they not only tried to buy johnson pills but got scammed in the process. They'll think it will make them look stupid and weak at the same time. And then the third type of unsatisfied customer... we'll give them a refund. We'll make enough profit from the other two that it'll barely be a drop in the bucket."

Tinker still hadn't been convinced. But Lafitte finally talked her into doing a trial run. They'd run the ads for one month. If the profits weren't through the roof by the end of four weeks, Lafitte promised to pull up stakes and repay Tinker out of her cut.

It had only taken two weeks for Tinker to see the potential in the con. They were soon receiving bags from the postman, who had given up trying to fit every order in their mailbox. The bank tellers quickly learned their names and braced when they saw Tinker or Lafitte coming in the door with the latest batch of checks. They ended up only charging five dollars for one bottle of pills, but they could produce a hundred bottles for under a buck.

After a year, Tinker could barely keep track of their profits. She knew their bank account, under false identities of course, was fit to bursting. And just as Lafitte had promised, the refund demands were few and far between and very easily subtracted from the pile of their riches.

It was snowing on Wednesday, the day Tinker always took the

week's earnings to be deposited. She was bundled up in her coat and hat, worried the bank might not even be open due to the storm. She was so distracted that she barely even noticed the man leaning against the building up ahead. It wasn't unusual to see other people at this hour of the morning, even in weather this lousy, so she didn't even look up as she passed him. Her mind barely even registered his existence until he was suddenly walking alongside on her left. He grabbed her left arm with his left hand, jerked her toward him, and pressed his right hand hard against her side.

The barrel of his gun was unmistakable, even through her layers of clothes.

"Keep walking, little girl," he said.

The voice scared her more than the gun. She clenched her jaw and kept her eyes forward. The snow on the sidewalk was unmarred, pristine, until they broke through it with their shuffling steps. Despite the wind chill, she started sweating under her coat. She could feel the sweat freezing on her brow as she finally looked to confirm she hadn't just been hearing things and saw the familiar profile. It was her own profile, just a bit rougher and with a nose that had once been broken and healed poorly.

Her father.

"No hello for your daddy?" He chuckled and the laugh came out on a plume of white. "I guess I can understand. Been a long time, hasn't it. Just keep walking, we're almost there."

Tinker scanned the area for potential escape routes. Barring that, she tried to see anything she might be able to use as a weapon. The damn snow had covered everything, preventing her from seeing any stone or loose brick that might have been her salvation. She was almost certain he was bluffing with the gun, but she couldn't take the chance it was actually loaded.

"The only reason you're still breathing is because I know you've only got checks in that bag. I need you to deposit them, and then to withdraw everything you've got in that fat account of yours. And if necessary, I can force your partner to do it instead. Keep that thought clear in your head, kid."

He walked her into a park, guiding her to a gazebo which looked ominous and otherworldly in the swirling snow. The wood was dark, and the ornate carving around the posts looked like some impossible to read symbology. He shoved her up the three steps and then followed her up. The snow had dusted a ring around the benches that ringed the interior, but the center was untouched.

Tinker turned to face him. She crossed her arms over her chest and aimed for an expression of indifference and anger. Anything to hide the fear she actually felt.

It had been over ten years since she'd last seen him. His cheeks were more hollow, his eyes sunken. He'd clearly had a rough decade, but she didn't feel any pity for him. He kept his arms down, but the gun at his waist was aimed steadily at her. He was planted between her and the only exit from the gazebo, but she was already trying to decide how risky it would be to vault the waist-high walls around the perimeter.

"Wonderin' how I found ya?" he asked, clearly impatient for her to ask.

Tinker shrugged.

He sucked on his teeth. "Victim of success, kiddo. Folks heard about your pecker pill scheme. A couple of fellas up in Michigan are copycatting you, even. Plenty of limp noodles around to share the wealth, probably." He wiped his hand under his nose. "Rumors were going around that a couple of ladies were running this one. One old, one young. Ladies are rare in this business, you know, so I had a couple folks sniff around. Lo and behold what they found. So how much you two figure you've earned so far?"

She stared at him. Every muscle was tensed so she wouldn't shiver. She didn't want to give him the satisfaction of thinking it was because of him.

He stepped forward. "You *owe* me, kiddo. You think that old hag is your mentor? I taught you everything you know about this game! If it wasn't for me, you'd be... you'd..." He waved the gun. "I saved your life. You could've been drowned in a ditch somewhere, but I took you in. Ruined my goddamn life doing it, too. So I think I'm entitled to a taste."

"Entitled to a taste?" Tinker hissed. "You made me sleep in a *fucking* closet for my entire childhood. You only thought about giving me a real bedroom when you decided I was old enough to sell to your friends. You're *entitled* to being shot in the gut and left to rot."

He bared his teeth. One was missing on the right side. "You watch your tone!"

Now that she'd broken her silence, she found it hard to stop. She moved closer to him. "What did you do, roll into town and stalk us? Figure out our schedule? That's on me. It was stupid to do the bank run on the same day every week." She shook her head at herself. "Sloppy. I guess I brought this on myself. So...? What's the plan, Father? Shoot me in the knee if I refuse to empty our bank account for you? Cut off a finger?"

"Maybe I'll cut off pieces of that old crone you're traveling with. A finger for every hour you don't come through with the cash."

Tinker laughed. "Oh. Oh, please. Yes, go after Lafitte. I would *love* to see you try to overwhelm her with... well, with anything, really. She's stronger than you. More clever than you. So unless you plan to walk up behind her and put a bullet in her head, I really don't see any world where you come out on top against her."

He sneered. "You're being awful mouthy for someone with a gun aimed at you."

"I'm pretty confident that gun is empty, Pop. And even if it's not, and you did shoot me, I'm sure the cop over there who seems pretty curious about the gun could get me to a doctor before things got too bad."

He spun in the direction she had nodded, scanning the swirling snow for the policeman. The only weapon Tinker had was the pen she always took to the bank to sign the deposit slip. She lunged at her father and jabbed the pen hard into the bicep of his dominant arm. She shoved her weight into him, herding him to the right until he slammed into one of the support beams. The impact made him lose his grip on the gun, and she was able to easily snatch it away from him.

"You stupid cu~"

She shot him in the foot.

He howled and fell to the floor of the gazebo, his entire body tense with pain. He was sputtering and screaming incoherently. She assumed whatever he was trying to say was insulting to her in some way or another, so she didn't try very hard to decipher it.

"Oh. So the gun *was* loaded, and I guess I was just imagining the cop. That's disappointing." She checked the gun to see how many more bullets were in it, then she tucked it into her coat pocket. "I'll try to do better the next time you darken my door. See ya, Pops." She looked at his bloody foot. "Assuming you get that taken care of, that is."

She left the gazebo, waiting until she was a fair distance away before she started running. Someone had to have heard the gunshot. The snow might make locating the source difficult, but she knew he would be found sooner rather than later.

She needed to get back to the office. She needed to explain everything to Lafitte, needed to get to the bank and clear their accounts. They needed to get the hell out of Marietta, Georgia, and go somewhere her father could never track her down again. From now on, it didn't matter where she was or how well she was doing.

She was never going to set down roots again.

Chapter Fourteen

ALBUQUERQUE
Friday July 13, 1945

Tinker found a town about a hundred miles south of Albuquerque with a gas station, an all-night diner, and an alley where she could park the truck where it wouldn't be seen from the street. She spent the night in a booth at the diner, her back to the wall so she could see the front windows and main entrance. She kept the clerk happy by placing a fifty on the table and asking him to keep the coffee flowing.

A placemat on the table explained the town was named Ferron after the man who founded it. The town boomed for a while after his discovery of gold, silver, and uranium deposits in the area and a handful of people hit it rich. Unfortunately the mines were quickly depleted and Ferron soon began bleeding its population. Its population was currently "forty strong" as of the time the placemat was printed.

The coffee kept her awake through the night. In the morning clerk made her a surprisingly delicious breakfast of biscuits and gravy, and she had two servings while she considered her next move.

The revival began on Sunday, which meant Riggs would probably arrive on Saturday to begin setting up. It gave her a day to get back to town, retrieve Chaplin, and get the hell out of there before he found them. But she had to consider Osker and his sidekick hung around for a while to see if she doubled back. How long could they linger before they had to be back in Santa Fe to help pack up and move the revival? They would probably have to leave by noon.

It would take about two hours to get back to Albuquerque if she took her time. When she decided to head out, she left a big tip for the clerk for letting her take over the booth, even though the place had never had more than five customers at any one time. She filled up her tank at the gas station and got a cold drink for the road.

She stayed well below the speed limit for the entire drive north, so it ended up taking her nearly three hours. Her truck rolled into town just before one o'clock, and she kept an eye on every side street, filling station, and alley for signs of the little Nash that had followed her from Santa Fe. She drove a figure-eight through town until she was satisfied they had moved on, and only then did she head toward Sophia's house.

Chaplin was out the front door of the main house before Tinker could even get out of the truck. She hurried across the lawn and they met halfway up the driveway.

"Where the hell have you been?" Chaplin asked.

Tinker looked past her at the closed front door. "Where's Sophia?"

"She had to go to work."

"What were you doing in the house while she was at work?"

Chaplin shook her head. "It's not important. Were you avoiding me?"

Tinker put her hand on Chaplin's arm. "Come on. Inside. We've got to pack everything and go."

"What?" Chaplin let herself be led. "You told me I had until Sunday to prove~"

"I know what I said, things changed." She threw open the guest house door and went straight to the bedroom. "I went up to Santa Fe to scout the revival. And it's a good fucking thing I did. Riggs is their guest pastor."

Chaplin went pale. "What? That's not possible."

"It's not only possible, they found me first. Osker was waiting in the truck. He grabbed me. They held me hostage in a hotel room for a few hours."

Somehow Chaplin managed to lose even more color. "No."

Tinker threw the dirty clothes she'd gathered onto the bed. "It was all a trick, obviously. They knew I'd get away and expected I'd lead them straight to you. But I outsmarted them. Led Osker and another goon out into the desert and convinced them to cut it out. Then I spent the night in a ghost town so they wouldn't catch me coming back."

Chaplin was starting to recover from the shock. "Well. Okay. No, this can be good. He's a known entity, right? We've humiliated him twice." She chuckled. "It might be fun to do it again."

"No, it won't." She stopped packing and faced Chaplin. "This time he knows we're here, he'll be ready for us. And not only that, he's been busy since the last time. He found my father."

Chaplin's eyes widened. "No."

"He sent him a telegram or called him, and the old man is probably on an express train here as we speak. He'll probably be here in a few hours. I intend to be as far away as possible when that happens. You're more than welcome to join me."

Chaplin looked toward the door, then at the duffel bag Tinker had started shoving things into. "We can't just leave."

"Why not? We already paid her rent for the whole month. We'll leave a note or something."

"We can't just leave a note."

"We'll just be those nice sisters who stayed with her for a few days and then vanished. It will be fine. We'll..." She stopped packing and looked at Chaplin. "Unless there's a reason she'll remember something different about us."

Chaplin rubbed a hand over her mouth and looked away. Then she looked back at Tinker, who deduced what the silence meant.

"Damn it, Penny. You were supposed to get to know her, not fuck her!"

"It wasn't something I planned. I don't think she planned it, either. It just felt right. You weren't here, and..." She shrugged. "I thought we had a little more time."

Tinker picked up a shirt Chaplin had left on the floor and tossed it to her. "Well, we don't. Pack. We're leaving *now*."

Chaplin looked down at the shirt. Finally, she said, "Okay. Okay, you're right. If your father and Riggs are coming to be here, we can't stay. But at least let me leave a note for Sophia so we don't just vanish on her."

"Fine," Tinker grunted. "Just don't take too long."

She finished packing her bag and looked around to make sure she hadn't left any of her things behind. They'd always traveled light, so it didn't take her long to confirm she had everything. She slung the strap of the bag over her shoulder and brushed past Chaplin, who was already looking for paper and pen to write her stupid note.

She fumed as she carried the bag out to the truck. She threw it into the back, then rested her hands against the side as if she needed it to support her. The metal was scorching hot from spending so long on the road, but she didn't let go. It reminded her of the furnace in Santa Fe, of scorching herself as she got the keys away from Vernon. She fought to get away, to get here to warn Chaplin, and then the stupid girl didn't even want to go? The ingratitude was galling, and it tightened her chest to the point where she was afraid she wouldn't be able to draw breath.

Chaplin had known that stupid woman for all of three days before jumping into bed with her. Before she was willing to risk everything to stick around. And who knew if it was going to be safe to leave the note? Riggs was persistent and lucky. He knew their fake names. If he was dogged enough to sniff around, what if he found this place? They couldn't risk it.

She wouldn't let Chaplin risk everything for anyone, especially not some woman she'd just met.

Chaplin found some stationary in the drawer and sat down at the kitchen counter, struggling to come up with a way to start the note. She'd never had to think about saying goodbye to anyone they'd left behind. She didn't know what was different about Sophia. The sex had been great, but she'd had great sex before. And she'd slept with women that she had to leave behind when they fled town. But she'd never given it a second thought until now. Until Sophia. In a way, she didn't blame Tinker for being irritated. Chaplin was the one acting different, the one who was insisting on a switch-up. If Riggs was on the way, they needed to be as gone as they could be. And if he was bringing Tinker's father along, they absolutely had to get disappeared.

So why was she delaying? Because of some woman who smiled nicely at her, who treated her well, who seemed alone and isolated...

"Damn it," Chaplin muttered.

She pulled out a stool and sat down. She would just start writing and see what came out.

Sophia,

I'm so sorry it has to be this way. The timing must look horrible. I knew we would have to leave soon, but I thought we would at least have a few days before it happened. I definitely thought you and I would have a chance for a proper goodbye. I hate leaving immediately after we went to bed. It must look callous and cruel. But things happened and everything's out of my control. If I want to be safe, I have to leave town immediately. If it was just me, I would risk it. At least for a few hours, for a chance to do this properly. But ~~Ti~~ Edith is also in danger, and I can't put her in danger for selfish reasons. I hope one day we're able to come back around this way, but that's a promise I can't make. I hope this isn't goodbye forever but, if it is, I'm very glad I got to know you.

All my love,

She stared at the bottom line of the page. She had crossed out her mistake where she had almost written Tinker's real name, but she didn't know how to sign it for herself. She didn't want to sign it as Margaret. That was a lie, a deception. Did she really want to end their acquaintance on a lie? But if she signed it as Penny Chaplin, it revealed that the very foundation of everything they'd said was a lie. That absolutely seemed worse.

Tinker appeared in the doorway. "Are you done? Can we go?"

"I'm done." Chaplin signed 'Someone who cares for you.' Then she folded the note twice and slipped off the stool. "What about the elixir?"

"We'll call it a loss. I'm not loading all that shit into the truck." She was already walking back toward the driveway. "Come on."

Chaplin jogged to the back door of the house. She opened it, leaned in, and placed the letter on the counter. She propped it up against the breadbox so hopefully Sophia would see it as soon as she came in from work. She hated leaving this way, wanted to actually explain at least part of why they had to leave in such a rush. But Tinker had already started the truck, its engine growling as if it was also angry at Chaplin, and she didn't dare push her luck.

She hurried to the truck. Tinker started backing up before Chaplin had even closed the door.

"Thank you for letting me leave the note," she said.

Tinker kept her eyes on the road ahead. "No more revivals. It's too fucking risky."

Chaplin wanted to fight back, wanted to argue, but she understood there was no way she would win this fight. So instead she nodded, said, "Okay," and looked out the window.

She only risked conversation when they were out of the town limits. "Where are we heading next?"

"I don't know," Tinker said. "West."

Chaplin nodded. "Okay. West."

They had been moving steadily westward the entire time they'd been partners, so it wasn't a surprise. From Philly to Virginia, down to Georgia and then across the South with a few detours here and there to keep things interesting. So it wasn't a surprise that Tinker wanted to stick with their unofficial route. But something she'd never thought about was the fact they would eventually run out of country. In just a few hundred miles they'd reach the coast and have to decide whether they wanted to turn north or circle back the way they had come.

She glanced at Tinker, who kept her eyes straight ahead, her brow furrowed.

For the first time Chaplin had to wonder if the end of their current road was more literal than she'd ever thought.

INTERLUDE

BROOKLYN, NEW YORK
Saturday, August 26, 1939

Laffite had been quiet since they left the World's Fair, something that had gotten more common in the past few months, but it still made Tinker uncomfortable. Silence meant something was wrong, something had been screwed up. Part of it was due to the fact they'd only been at the fair to pick pockets and do a handful of amateur parlor tricks. Laffite wasn't as quick as she'd once been. She couldn't run, couldn't think as fast on her feet, and her fumbling had cost them more than one payday. But being reduced to a pickpocket hurt her pride, Tinker knew. It was undeniable proof of how far she'd declined.

Tinker didn't mind the small jobs. They were as important as the bigger cons, the jobs in which she was starting to take a leading role. And that was fine with her. Laffite had earned her promotion to a management role. She could just sit in the hotel and orchestrate the con while Tinker went out and did the heavy lifting, the sweating. It was high time she'd become the face of their partnership. Laffite needed to get comfortable being the mastermind.

None of this was anything Tinker could actually say to Laffite's face, of course. Any attempts resulted in anger, thrown glassware, accusations that Tinker just wanted to cut her out completely.

So Tinker had learned to match silence with silence, and neither of them said a word on the way back to the hotel.

Laffite took off her boater hat as she walked into the room, tossing it onto the bed as she walked to the armchair. She walked like every step hurt her, like her whole body ached. When she dropped down into the seat, she let out a weary sigh and pushed a hand through her shaggy hair.

"Well? Aren't you going to say it?"

Tinker feigned ignorance. "We've had better days, I suppose."

Laffite snorted a laugh and shook her head. "Oh, lord. I'm getting old. I fumbled at least six wallets today. And three of the ones I did manage to keep a grip on, I would've gotten caught if you weren't there to play the distraction."

"We cover each other's backs," Tinker said. "That's how it's always been."

"Always been," Laffite echoed. "Over twenty years, did you realize that? You were just a kid then. Now look at you. All grown up and pulling my fat out of the fryer every damn time."

Tinker sighed. "It's just summer, Fee. Everyone was sluggish out there today. Once the seasons turn, you'll be back in your sweet spot."

"You're sweet. But I'm just admitting what you've been thinking for months. My time is done."

"No."

Laffite shook her head. "It's true. If I can't even slip a wallet out of some rube's pocket, what use am I gonna be in another six months? I'll be tripping over my words in December and you'll just say 'oh it's cold out, once the weather warms up, you'll be your old self again in no time.' And you'll be as wrong then as you are now."

"Okay. Well, if I've been saying this for so long, what finally made you agree with me?"

"Television." Laffite's eyes bugged out and she shook her head. "Did you see that thing? They televised a baseball game, aired it right there on the show floor. It was like I had a seat in the stadium."

Tinker couldn't believe what she was hearing. "That? You were impressed by that? Every time someone swung the bat, it was just a muddy blur. You couldn't even see the ball most of the time!"

Laffite laughed. "Welcome to my world, kid. Someone moves too fast, it's just a muddy blur. And I gave up on seeing the ball a *long* time ago. As far as I'm concerned, that television was the exact same experience I would have gotten live. Better, even. And if that's the world we're going into... it's not a world I know. Things are changing too fast for me. I can't... I don't know how to move around in a world where someone can zap a baseball game all over the country like that."

Tinker lowered her head. "That doesn't mean anything. You want to start planning the jobs while I go out to do them, fine, we'll do that. But stop talking like you're some relic that needs to be put on a shelf."

"I'm only talking that way because that's exactly what I am. You know my gift. I see things the way they are. Or at least I used to." She chuckled and gestured at her eyes. "If I lose that, I lose who I am. I don't want to be anyone else."

Tinker's eyes burned with tears. "I don't like what you're saying."

"I'd be horribly offended if you did, darling." She laughed under her breath. "If you listened to this and jumped for joy, I would get up and slap you across the face. But it's time. It really is time."

"So what happens to me?"

"You keep doing what we've been doing. Hell, you've been carrying me the past few years anyway. You're good, kid. Hell, if you want brutal honesty, you're better than I was when we first met. You were born with talent and you've added skill on top of it. That's a killer combination. Just keep moving and stay on your toes. You'll be fine."

"I don't want to do this alone."

"Then get a partner."

Tinker shook her head. "I meant~"

"I know what you meant." Laffite sighed and leaned forward, elbows on her knees. "If you stick with me, I'm going to get you caught. I'll fumble or screw up and call you the wrong name. Something. And what happens after that is going to hurt a hell of a lot more than this does right now. And no one does this sort of thing forever."

Tinker looked at Laffite. "I'm scared."

"Good. Scared keeps you on your toes." She reached out and patted Tinker's arm. "You'll do fine, kid. Just fine. And one day you're going to find some punk with more skill than smarts, and you're going to take her under your wing. You'll pass it on down the line. We're all just one big chain."

She stood up and bent down to kiss the top of Tinker's head. Tinker looked up at her.

Laffite smiled and winked.

"Go find the next link, kid."

Chapter Fifteen

FLAGSTAFF, ARIZONA
Friday July 13, 1945

They drove almost nonstop for five hours, stopping only so they could walk out into the scrub alongside the road for the call of nature. Neither of them admitted it out loud, but they both half-expected the other to use the opportunity to drive off. Neither would have done that, just abandoned the other out in the desert over what was basically an argument. But Chaplin made sure she checked over her shoulder frequently, and Tinker made sure she had the keys in her pocket when she walked away from the truck.

The first true stop they made was in Flagstaff, for gas. A new state, a new city, and a whole new start for them. Tinker hoped it was the first step in putting Albuquerque behind them. They'd had a fight. Chaplin had gotten laid. They'd had a near miss with Riggs. They lost the potential income from the revival, but the grocery store con had more than made up for it.

Albuquerque would go down as a success. She was certain of it. And once Chaplin got over being sore, once she realized Sophia was just the latest in a long line of brief flings, she would be back to her usual self instead of the sullen, silent lump currently brooding against the passenger door.

Tinker had gotten out to open the tank, and now she leaned into the open driver's side window. "Well, you going to head inside and pay?"

Chaplin looked at the other car parked at the pumps. It had seen better days. Dented fender, door held on by a rope looped around the window.

"I'm not stealing from whoever is driving that."

Tinker rolled her eyes. "No one is asking you to, princess. No sin to pay full price when you can afford it. G'wan, they won't turn it on until you cough up the coin."

Chaplin slowly got out of the truck.

"Is this how it's going to be from now on?" Tinker asked. "You just assuming the worst of me at every turn?"

"You're the one who decided the rules don't matter."

"And you're the one who decided that bending the rules every now and then is fine and dandy," Tinker snapped, surprised at her own sudden anger.

Chaplin blinked, surprised, then looked away. "I..."

"Just go pay."

Chaplin turned away and went into the station. Tinker rubbed her face and went to the pump. She wanted to punch something, kick something, but she didn't want to make a scene. Instead, she grabbed a handful of her hair and pulled hard, growling at the tingling pain in her scalp. She took the nozzle from the pump and jammed it into the tank, then walked out toward the road as it filled. The landscape didn't look much different from Albuquerque. The hills were bigger and the scrub was more green, but it was still a whole lot of empty nothing.

She was still staring west when Chaplin appeared next to her. Tinker looked over, and Chaplin held out a bag of jelly beans.

Tinker looked at the bag, then at Chaplin, who was staring straight ahead. After a moment, Tinker took the bag and ripped it open.

"I'm sorry. About Tulsa."

"It was Oklahoma City." Tinker popped a purple jelly bean into her mouth and chewed slowly.

Chaplin said, "Wherever it was. I thought if we just got it out of the way..."

Tinker sighed. "It's not your fault. I thought the same thing." The tension faded from her shoulders. She looked down into the bag and jostled it, looking for another purple. "That's how it usually happens. Get it out of your system, right? Scratch the itch, those pesky feelings go away, you can move on. It's not your fault I just got more hung up on you."

"Mm. And I... I wish I felt the same way about you."

"I don't." She looked at Chaplin. "Honestly. Part of what makes me so angry is knowing that what I want is unreasonable. You care about me. I know you do. That should be enough to make anyone happy. I'm grateful you're in my life, Penny. Wishing for something more is like saying what we have isn't enough. It is. You're the best partner I could've asked for. And I hate myself for getting so angry about you drawing a line."

Chaplin was silent. "We could have sex from time to time, if it would help."

Tinker laughed.

"I'm serious! You're pretty good at it." She shrugged. "I've screwed people I like less for worse reasons. It could just be a thing we do."

Tinker shook her head and popped another jelly bean. "I think that would just make things worse, Penny. But I appreciate the offer."

They stayed by the road until the gas tank was full, then left the gas station behind them. Flagstaff seemed like it was still too close to Albuquerque to even consider setting up another job, so they drove on through and kept going. Tinker intended to get all the way to California before they even started looking for a new place to put down stakes.

"I was thinking..." Tinker cleared her throat, looked at Chaplin, and then adjusted her hands on the steering wheel. It was sticky from the sun beating down on it. Part of her wondered if it was leaving black marks on her fingers from holding it so long. "When we hit the coast, we need to make some decisions."

"What kind of decisions?"

Tinker shrugged. "We've just been going west ever since we met. I mean, essentially, with some meandering. We've been going to California this whole time. We're only about seven hours from there now. So if we set up in a new town, we should talk about where we're going next in case we have to make another speedy escape like the one we just made. Have you given any thought to that?"

Chaplin rubbed her hand over her chin. She looked out the window as if she could see a map laid out over the land.

"Well," she said slowly. "I figured we would just follow the road. Go north. I don't like the idea of turning around, especially with Riggs and your father back there looking for us. And there's a lot less audience for those revivals once you get a little more north."

"True."

"And it might be nice to be somewhere it rains once in a while."

Tinker nodded. "Okay. So no more desert. Mountains."

"Forests."

"Rivers."

Chaplin grinned.

Tinker relaxed. She was relieved that it seemed like the tension between them had faded. Albuquerque had just been a cursed town, a bad idea from the jump. They'd lined their pockets very nicely and now they could start over in a new town. In a few weeks, Chaplin probably wouldn't even remember Sophia or the argument they'd had because of her.

She breathed in deeply and let the air out slowly. It was the nature of the con. Don't carry more than you needed to carry, and move on when things got too tight.

If they could get over this bump, they could go on to have a very productive partnership.

Chaplin put her hat over her eyes and tried to get some sleep while Tinker drove. She offered to take the wheel for a few hours, but Tinker said it wasn't necessary. She hadn't gotten any quality sleep the night before, Chaplin knew, but she claimed the road helped keep her focused. Chaplin wasn't going to argue. She was still exhausted from her night with Sophia.

She was more than happy to let Tinker think Albuquerque was dead, buried, and forgotten behind them. But the truth was that it felt like an elastic band was tied around her chest. The other end was bolted to the side yard of Sophia's house. It felt like it could snap her back at any moment, and she would welcome the return.

Chaplin had seen the cracks and knew they were heading straight for disaster. She knew Tinker would never change her position or admit she was wrong. If she kept pushing, everything would shatter. They'd be broken forever and they'd never collect all the pieces. So standing in the gas station, stating into the icebox, she decided to fall on her sword for the good of the partnership.

She wasn't blameless, after all. She'd gotten too close to

Sophia. She'd gone to bed with Tinker. She'd let her urges take control and made bad decisions because of it.

She got the jelly beans as an olive branch. She hoped time would make Tinker realize her brash behavior in Albuquerque was due to hurt feelings and she would quietly go back to their old rules, their original agreement. Trying anything else was dangerous. Poor people were desperate, could react violently to someone trying to steal from them. She didn't want to risk that on top of the morality of stealing from someone who needed the money to survive.

The only thing she knew for certain was that they couldn't let the partnership dissolve. Tinker didn't know, but two years ago, Chaplin had gone to the library and dug through old newspapers to see what she could find about Tinker's former partner, Laffite. It was supposed to be a nice surprise, a bit of information to drop when Tinker was feeling low. Instead, she ended up with a terrible secret that she hoped Tinker never learned.

According to the papers, Laffite had only lasted two months after she parted ways with Tinker. She was found dead in a sleeper car of a train upon its arrival in New Orleans. Other passengers had seen her drinking almost nonstop the night before during a card game with a man no one seemed able to describe. They testified she'd probably drank enough to be fatal, but she had been killed with three stab wounds to the abdomen. Her pockets were empty, and her single piece of luggage hadn't contained a single red penny.

She'd died penniless and drunk, abandoned in a train car by the man who robbed her, and the newspaper hadn't even bothered to print her real name. The only time she was named at all was in the first line: "The local confidence artist known as Laffite was found dead today aboard a train coming from Philadelphia." The last line said she'd been buried in a pauper's grave.

Chaplin had no idea how she would even begin to share that information with Tinker. Her mentor had cut ties and then wound up dead and destitute trying to go home.

She knew there would come a time when she and Tinker parted ways. Their roads were bound to split sooner or later. All she could do was make sure Tinker was in a good place when that happened. She was determined to keep their partnership alive as long as it took to be sure she was safe.

CHAPTER SIXTEEN

SAN DIEGO, CALIFORNIA
Sunday July 15, 1945

They arrived in San Diego after dark. Tinker drove the entire way, twelve full hours with only a handful of stops. The silence only lasted a few more miles after the gas station stop. Chaplin tested the waters by starting to sing a song and Tinker joined her at the chorus. They spent the next few hours as their own radio, butchering lyrics and making up their own versions of songs that they half remembered from the movies.

They drove to the ocean since it was too late to find anywhere reputable to stay. They had enough for a hotel, but neither of them made the suggestion. The truck was scorching from the hours spent driving in the hot sun and they rolled down the windows to let it out and the ocean breeze in. Tinker slumped down behind the wheel. Chaplin put her back to the door and stretched out along the seat, crossing her feet in Tinker's lap. Tinker put her hand on Chaplin's ankle and looked over at her.

"What do you think?" she asked. "Are we going to stick with the Byrds?"

Chaplin shook her head. "Riggs would recognize it. I don't think California is a big market for their revivals, but you never know. Probably best for us to be someone else. Sophia never bought that we were sisters anyway."

Tinker scoffed. "Well, I'm not pretending to be your mother. Even if I am old enough for it to be true."

"Maybe if you had me young."

Tinker laughed. "Go to sleep. We'll figure out who we are tomorrow."

"Good night, Tinker."

The next day, they found a place where they could stay for a while under the names Eleanor Taylor and Florence Morris. Their backstory was that Tinker, Eleanor, was the widow of a newspaper mogul visiting from New York. Chaplin, Florence, would be her assistant. They spent Saturday relaxing and getting used to their new identities, scouring the local media for potential targets. They were close enough to Hollywood for some of the more desperate fame-seekers to drift onto their radar, and the town was touristy enough that victims would be arriving in droves every day.

On Sunday, Tinker went out to establish herself in the city. It didn't take a lot of work. Figuring out where to drink, being seen there with a glass in her hand, introducing herself to the right people who would then whisper her name in the right car. They had to be sure they weren't stepping on anyone's toes or poaching in established territory so they didn't ruffle anyone's feathers.

Chaplin stayed in the hotel room while Tinker did the handshake work. The less anyone saw of her, the better. She needed to keep her face as unknown as possible just in case anonymity was required later. She needed to maintain the ability to become whoever the situation required. It was a necessary evil, but it was also mind-numbingly boring.

After eating the lunch she'd had delivered to the room, she remembered Tinker had a novel stashed away somewhere. She dug through the bags they'd brought up and didn't find it, so she went downstairs to the truck. It wasn't in the glove compartment, under the seat, or anywhere in the cab, so she started digging around in their bag of tricks tied in the bed of the truck.

Sophia Ellis' pocket watch was sitting on top of their ingredients for the elixir.

Chaplin stared at it, refusing to accept the version of events her brain was putting together. She reached down and lifted it. She remembered the way it felt in her palm, the weight of the thing. Her thumb brushed over the engraved face of its cover. There was no denying what it was, so she also couldn't deny how it had gotten there.

She could see the entire sequence of events clearly. She'd sat down at the kitchen counter to write her goodbye note to Sophia. Tinker had gone out to load the truck. And while Chaplin sat there trying to figure out the exact right thing to say, Tinker had slipped into the house and taken the watch from the bookshelf. Chaplin kicked herself for not thinking it strange the door had been unlocked when she left the note on the counter. And she was the one who told Tinker that Sophia wasn't home, so the theft would go unnoticed.

"You bitch," she whispered, curling her fingers around the pocket watch. Her eyes burned with tears. She balled her other hand into a fist and punched the side of the truck hard enough to send shockwaves of pain up her arm. Her knuckles left a sizeable crater in the metal as well. She was breathing so hard that someone might have thought she'd just finished running a lap around the building.

Her face burned with rage, but she forced herself to think. It was Sunday. July fifteenth. The revival was in Albuquerque. Riggs was there. So was Tinker's father. If she went back, she would literally be sticking her hand into a flame and hoping it didn't burn her.

Chaplin looked down at the watch.

She made her decision.

Tinker got back to the hotel around five o'clock, exhausted from the shows she'd been forced to put on for everyone in town. But she'd gotten a handful of good leads, and she expected Chaplin would have a lot of good ideas for how to go after the potential victims. Hollywood was such a big draw, and the people orbiting that town were eager to believe any kind of luck or chance that dropped into their laps. She hoped Chaplin wouldn't bristle at the idea of targeting young and impressionable creative types. She might have to find some charitable angle.

"We're showing them how unlikely their dreams are before they waste years they can't get back," she said under her breath as she walked back to the hotel. "We're saving them. If they have to run home and get a real job, they'll thank us in a few years when they..." She trailed off as she let herself into the room. "Penny? I'm back."

She glanced around the room and assumed Chaplin had gone out to get dinner. She took off her hat and sunglasses, then noticed the sheet of paper left in the middle of one bed. She walked over, craning her head to read the angled letters.

YOU LYING BITCH.
I'M TAKING IT BACK TO HER.

Tinker's whole body went cold. She ran to the window and shoved the curtains aside to look down into the parking lot. Their truck was gone. She slapped her palm against the wall hard. "Damn it, Chaplin!"

She started to leave the room, but she stopped when she realized she had no idea where she would go. There was nowhere to go, nothing she could do. Chaplin had their only vehicle, and she had a head start of who knew how long. She could already be a hundred miles away. Tinker paced in front of the beds and tried to consider her options, her hand shaking as she ran it over her face.

Tinker was furious with herself for not keeping the watch in her pocket. She had always planned to confess about what she'd done. But not yet, not when the whole Sophia situation was still a fresh wound. In a few days, after they had a few more successful cons under their belts, when Albuquerque was in the past, Tinker would reveal what she'd done. It was supposed to be a nest egg, insurance for a bad run. "This will buy us a week, maybe a month, where we don't have to worry about where our next meal is coming from. We can just take a train somewhere and relax for a change."

Now there was no chance Chaplin would listen to reason. And the longer it took Tinker to figure out what the hell she was going to do, the more impossible it would be to catch up with Chaplin. She grabbed her hat and sunglasses and ran from the room, hoping a plan would materialize by the time she got downstairs.

Her answer was waiting outside the hotel at the curb. A 1940 Lincoln Continental sat gleaming and ready, as if someone had put it there specifically for her. It was nicer than their truck and, more importantly, more streamlined and built for speed. She'd never beat Chaplin back to Albuquerque but, if she pushed it hard, there was a chance she could catch up to her.

The windows were down due to the heat, so she unlocked the door and climbed in. The keys were still in the ignition, a further sign that this was meant to be. She didn't bother looking around to see if anyone had noticed her. People would only pay attention if she acted suspicious. If she acted normally, she would just look like a woman heading out for a drive.

She adjusted the seat, checked for traffic, and pulled away from the curb. She waited until she was on a main stretch before she rested her weight on the accelerator. The speedometer climbed steadily, fifty miles per hour, then sixty, seventy. Their truck topped out there, but the Lincoln kept purring along. Eighty miles per hour, inching higher.

She had a chance. If she could just skip any unnecessary stops, if Chaplin hadn't left too long ago, maybe there was a chance Tinker could catch up with her and stop the disaster from unfolding.

Chapter Seventeen

OUTSIDE ALBUQUERQUE, NEW MEXICO
Before dawn, Monday July 16, 1945

Chaplin could barely keep her eyes open. She had been driving nonstop since she left San Diego, only stopping twice when her bladder threatened disaster. She had stocked up on water and food at the same time, killing two birds with one stone. It was somewhere after five in the morning, probably a few minutes before dawn, and she was almost at the end of her road. She refused to lag now.

She gripped the steering wheel with both hands at the twelve o'clock position, staring between them. When the ribbon of asphalt became too monotonous, she flexed her fingers and looked at the knuckles, her nails, anything to break up the unendingness of the road. The sun had gone down hours ago but the heat had remained. She had both windows down but the breeze wasn't doing much to cool the sweat on her face and throat.

She wanted to stop, wanted to go somewhere and get a big glass of ice water, but she didn't dare. She knew Tinker too well. She'd known what leaving the note would do. Tinker wouldn't see it as a "goodbye," she'd see it as "Come and get me." She didn't know how Tinker could possibly give chase without a car, but she also knew "impossible" wasn't a word Tinker allowed in her vocabulary.

Chaplin could see Albuquerque in the distance, a bright spot against the blackness of the desert, when her rearview mirror filled with a blinding light. She squinted up at it, then checked the side mirror. A car was coming up on her fast. She tightened her grip on the steering wheel, clenched her teeth, and pressed harder on the accelerator.

The car pulled into the passing lane and started gaining. She glanced over, but it was far too dark to see the driver. She didn't need confirmation, though. There was only one person who could possibly be driving on this road, at this moment. Chaplin tried to goose a little more speed but the truck was already pushing its limits. The car easily overtook her and pulled in front, then started to slow down.

"Damn it to hell," Chaplin muttered as she put on the brakes and pulled to the shoulder.

Tinker got out of the car but left the door standing open. Chaplin got out as well, meeting her halfway.

"Where'd you get the car?"

"Where do you think?" Tinker said. "I'm a thief. I take what I need. Are you going to judge me after you stole *our* truck?"

Chaplin said, "You took the watch."

"Of course I took the watch!" Tinker shouted. "I'm not going to just leave a payday like that sitting on the shelf."

"It's not your payday. It's hers. It's her family, it's~"

"She clearly has no idea~"

"You don't know that!"

Tinker shouted, "But I don't *care*. She's just a woman I'll never see again, in a town I'll probably never be in again."

"Didn't Riggs showing up teach you anything? And your father? Screw enough people and one of them will eventually catch up with you. The least we can do is minimize the awfulness we spread around."

"Only hurt the bad guys," Tinker said. "I have news for you, Penny. The bad guys are the ones most likely to come after you when they're pissed off."

"So only the people who have already been victimized. Take their last penny, leave them totally helpless. I think we both know what that feels like."

Tinker said, "And I have no intention of going back to it. That watch is a life preserver. It keeps us going. It keeps us alive."

Chaplin said, "So do unto others before they can do unto you, right?"

"If that's what it takes."

Chaplin pressed her hands against her face. "I don't know if that's who I want to be. If that's where we're going with this, just taking and not caring about anyone~"

"Caring for each other," Tinker said. "Because who else matters?"

"That is a bleak way to go through life, Tinker."

They stared at each other in the morning silence. Chaplin didn't know what else to say, certain that nothing she said would change Tinker's mind. But she also didn't want to walk away. Leaving would mean the fight was over, and that would mean they were really and truly finished. As angry as she might be, and despite the rage she'd felt when she left the note in San Diego, she didn't want to end things this way. She didn't want to end things at all. But she had no idea what else was left to be said.

Tinker suddenly looked past Chaplin, her brow furrowed in confusion. "What in the world is that?"

Chaplin rolled her eyes, refusing to look away. But then she saw something reflected in Tinker's eyes that made her pause. There was a light there, a bloom of bright yellow filling the irises.

"Sunrise," Chaplin said, hoping she sounded more certain than she felt.

"That's south." Tinker's voice was soft, almost reverent.

Chaplin turned around to look. The thing she saw was definitely not the sun, but she didn't know what else it could be. Then she felt it. The ground shook under her feet and the air was suddenly alive with a rumble coming from the direction of the light. That was when she realized she was looking at an explosion. A massive, unholy explosion bigger than anything she'd ever seen. It would have looked unbelievable in the middle of a city, but there was nothing out there. It was empty desert. What the hell could possibly have exploded out there...

She felt Tinker's hand on her shoulder. That simple touch was enough to bring tears to her eyes, and she reached out blindly. Tinker's other hand took hers, squeezed it.

"There's nothing out there," Tinker whispered.

"It was a bomb." Chaplin could only think of the war. She'd heard of awful weapons their enemies had been working on. She hadn't heard a plane engine, but maybe it was some kind of missile.

Whatever the source, she knew it had to be something man-made and evil. Someone had created a weapon that would make an explosion like that in a populated city. New York or London or...

The desert was silent now. The cloud of fire had dissipated but the sight was still burned on the back of Chaplin's eyes. She had a feeling it would never go away.

She let go of Tinker's hand. They stepped away from each other, as if time had reset itself. Chaplin couldn't think of anything she wanted to do less than continue their fight, but she didn't know what else to do.

"I don't know what happens now," she admitted.

"We take it back," Tinker said softly. "We give her the watch back."

Tinker looked smaller somehow. There was a pallor to her face that was visible even in the dim light, which alerted Chaplin to the fact the sun actually had started to rise in its proper place in the sky.

"Are you serious?" Chaplin was almost breathless with anger. "After all this, after chasing me across the damn desert, you just suddenly changed your mind?"

"Did we just see the same thing?" Tinker asked, pointing to the south.

"You don't even know what that was!"

"No," Tinker said, "and that is so much scarier. What are the odds it was the only one? What if there were more? In New York and Los Angeles and London and... and what if it's just the first?" She looked up at the sky. Chaplin looked too, but she only saw the same sweep of stars as usual. "Whatever that was, it wasn't natural or normal. I know you felt that, too. You know that was something horrible."

Chaplin swallowed. "So what does that change?"

"I don't know." She wiped the back of her hand across her cheek and Chaplin realized she was crying. "I saw it behind you. And it looked like it was coming out of you. And then I understood it was something else. I thought it would keep growing. I thought it was coming toward us, and I thought the last thing I'd do in this life is stand here fighting you. And I regretted it."

Chaplin's shoulders relaxed. She felt the anger fading from her as well. "We don't know what it was," she said again. "Maybe it was our side."

"That's not better," Tinker said. "If that's how we're fighting, it's only a matter of time before we're all... before everything..."

She sniffled and wiped her face again.

Chaplin looked back in the direction of the explosion. Everything looked calm and normal now.

"So maybe you're right," she said. "If the good guys are building weapons like that to fight the bad guys, then maybe everyone really is evil."

Tinker laughed. It was a flat sound, like dropping stones onto asphalt. "Great. We managed to convince each other of our arguments."

Chaplin laughed as well and rubbed her forehead. "Sophia deserves the watch. And whatever riches come from it."

"Okay," Tinker said. "I'm not willing to fight on that any more. All I care about is you, Penny. I didn't... I *don't* want you to think less of me. So if that's what you think is right, then... then... okay. You call the shots."

"Okay," Chaplin said quietly. She looked toward Albuquerque. "Riggs and your father are probably in town right now. Along with Osker and the whole crew. We'll have to be really careful not to be seen."

"You'll have to be careful," Tinker corrected. Her voice was distant, and her eyes were even farther away. Chaplin had seen the look before, when Tinker was forced to think fast and improvise on jobs gone wrong. "I'm... I have something else I need to do..."

Chaplin stepped closer to her. "Don't do anything crazy."

"Why would you think that?"

"Like you said, we saw the same thing out there." She pointed out into the desert. "I'm shaken. But you're suddenly talking like a completely different person. You just raced across the desert to catch me, and now you're giving up. You'll understand if I'm worried."

Tinker stepped forward and cupped Chaplin's face in her hands. She smiled at her. "I'm just thinking clearly," she said. "Twelve hours alone in a car and then whatever that was..." She nodded her chin to the south. "I suddenly realized why I was angry. And what I really want. Cut down to its bare bones, the only thing I want is to keep you safe. And take care of you."

"You have," Chaplin said softly.

"Good. Can..." She chewed her bottom lip and looked down at her shoes. "I've never pushed you for this, and I'll understand if you say no. But just in case we don't see each other again~"

"What?"

"I'd like to know your real name."

Chaplin blinked. She was still trying to process the possibility they wouldn't see each other again. "I-I don't... Penny Chaplin is my real name."

"I know. But. I just... I'd like to know. Just so I can know it. I want to be one of a handful of people who can say they knew you well enough to know the name you were born with."

Chaplin stared into Tinker's eyes. What she saw there was scarier than the unknown explosion. "What are you going to do in Albuquerque, Emilie?"

Tinker tensed, then laughed. "Well. See? You've already got a leg up on me."

"Don't do anything stupid."

"I haven't done anything stupid in decades. It's all part of the plan." She chuckled and kissed Chaplin's forehead. "I love you, Penny Chaplin."

"I love you, too."

Tinker started to walk away, but Chaplin grabbed her hand to pull her back. She stepped close, leaning in as if she was going for a kiss. Instead, her lips went to Tinker's ear. Her face was curtained by Tinker's dark hair when she whispered a name she hadn't said out loud since she was a child. Saying it, hearing herself say it, made something shake inside her chest. It felt like a physical cage being rattled against her ribs, and she was breathless when she took a step back.

"That's the name I was born with. You're the only person I've ever told. Ever."

Tinker touched Chaplin's face again. "Thank you, Penny."

She started walking toward her stolen car. Chaplin chased her.

"Tinker, *wait*. Don't~"

Tinker stopped and looked at the car, then she turned to look at the truck. She reached into the car and retrieved the keys, walked back, and handed them to Chaplin.

"Take it."

"What? Why? We're trading vehicles?"

Tinker ignored the question and went to the truck. She searched until she found the money they had stashed in the cushions and came back to Chaplin. She put the stack on top of the keys.

"That's yours."

"*Half* is mine," Chaplin corrected. "This is *our* stash, from *our* jobs. I'm not taking the whole thing. What are you~"

Tinker said, "Take it. Take the car. Go back to Sophia's house. The revival is set up on the southeast side of town." She went to the truck and checked to make sure the keys were in the ignition. "If you stick to the outskirts and go clockwise around the edge of town, you should be able to get to Sophia's without being seen by anyone associated with the church."

"Don't. Whatever you're planning, don't."

Tinker looked at her with such a calm, determined look, that Chaplin almost believed the next thing she said.

"This is the way it has to end, Chaplin. I've been turning it over in my mind since I left San Diego, trying to make it end different, and it ends bad every time. It ends with us running forever, or dead, or turning on each other. But I figured it out. I know how this ends. I know the payoff."

She got in the truck and slammed the door. Chaplin listened to the engine roar to life, the first sound they'd heard since the unidentified rumble. She knew there was no point in fighting, in continuing to argue. She'd gotten what she wanted, but she couldn't help but think the price for victory would be more than she was willing to pay.

Tinker pulled the truck away from the shoulder and weaved wide around the car. Chaplin watched her go, a fortune in one hand and the keys of her new stolen car in the other, and watched until the darkness swallowed the truck from view.

Dawn had fully broken by the time Chaplin pulled into Sophia's driveway. She had followed Tinker's advice and drove around the edge of the city. She didn't get anywhere near the revival, and also avoided motels, hotels, restaurants that were open for breakfast... anywhere Riggs and his cronies could conceivably be.

She wanted to stay in the car, but she knew Sophia had probably heard her pull up. So she got out, retrieved the watch from where she'd hidden it, and walked to the back door. She kept her head down when she knocked, then took a step back.

Sophia opened the door a few seconds after peeking through the curtain. Chaplin looked up at her and started to speak, but the explanation died on her tongue. Sophia was still in her pajamas under a robe that looked very comfy. She stared out at Chaplin with an odd, unreadable expression. Confused, angry, and hopeful all jockeyed for position in her eyes and the set of her mouth. Finally,

Chaplin knew she had to break the silence.

"I have a confession to make. My real name is Penny Chaplin. My partner's name is... she goes by Tinker." She pulled the watch out of her pocket and held it out. "We stole this from you."

Sophia looked at the watch. Confusion finally won out. "You brought it back."

Chaplin felt a dart in her chest. So she had noticed it was missing. Of course she had. "I told Tinker not to take it. We had a huge argument about it. And when we had to skip town, she took it without telling me. As soon as I found out she had it, I immediately got in the truck and–"

"You weren't supposed to bring it back."

Chaplin bit down on her rambling confession. It was her turn to look confused.

"I'm sorry, what...?"

Sophia stepped back and opened the door wider to let Chaplin come inside. She stepped in and put the watch on the counter before she turned to look at Sophia, who shut the door and drew the curtain shut over the window.

"What do you mean I wasn't supposed to bring it back?"

Anger had returned to the set of Sophia's jaw. Chaplin remembered the day they looked at the house, how brittle and sharp Sophia had seemed. She'd completely changed during their next conversation, a bright and friendly landlady who was more than willing to cook dinner for them. Sophia walked deeper into the kitchen.

"You're a con artist, right?" she said. "You're fucking thieves who can't resist having something shiny waved under your noses."

"You... knew?"

"Of course I knew. I'm not an idiot." She had been cooking breakfast, and she moved the pan to a cool burner. "I know a con when I see one. You and that other one, strolling in here, calling yourselves sisters? Is everyone you run into a damn moron?"

"What is going on?" Chaplin asked.

"It was a trap!" Sophia yelled. "The dinner invitation, the watch just sitting out in the open like that..." She rubbed her forehead. "I... I didn't expect the... other thing. I suppose you should know that. I really did start to like you that day. And I gave in. It's been a long time since I felt that relaxed around anyone. And I figured, hey, if I can get some sex out of the deal, why not go for it."

Chaplin tried to remember every moment they'd spent together, looking for tells she'd missed. There hadn't been anything. Except for her change of personality. It should have been the biggest red flag, but she'd just ignored it.

"The watch isn't fake," she said. "I know my watches."

"No, it's not fake," Sophia snapped. "The watch is very real. And every jeweler, pawn shop, and fence between here and California has a description of it. The second you tried to sell it, a flag would have gone up and you'd have been arrested within the hour."

Chaplin pulled a chair away from the dinner table and sat down. Her hands were shaking. "Why?"

"One of you assholes got your hooks in my mother before she died. Took her for everything she had. And when she got sick, oh! That was such a blessing! You love your miracle cures, don't you? I saw a whole icebox full of them in the guest house when you left. How many little old ladies do you think you've given false hope? How many of them stopped taking their medication because they had something 'even better' that had been delivered by miracle workers?"

"We..." Chaplin didn't have an argument.

"My mother died because someone sold her bottles of sugar water for ten dollars each. She died broke and in pain. She almost lost this house. I managed to save it, barely, but it almost ruined me, too. Then I found that watch. That priceless antique. It could save me. But it could also serve a purpose.

"Do you know that you and that other one were the third to take the bait? One man tried to pawn it in Kansas City. Another didn't even leave the state and took it to a guy in Santa Fe. Both times, the flag went up. The cops came in. I gave a report. And the watch came floating back to me. I suppose a side effect is that it taught me a little about why you do this. It's addictive. And thrilling. I needed the money but I didn't have anything else that was anywhere near as enticing to a thief. So I got a normal job to pay the bills, and I kept renting out the guest house, waiting for the next con to fall."

"You're good," Chaplin said. "I can usually spot a con from a mile away."

"Gee, thanks." Sophia looked down at her bare feet, then tucked her hair behind her ear. "I never went to bed with anyone else. I was never even tempted. But the day you played the piano for me, I forgot. I let myself forget. It was nice. And you're gorgeous. And I haven't been with anyone for so long. I would feel guilty, but you were lying to me, too. I didn't even know your real damn name."

Chaplin cleared her throat. "I'm sorry."

"Yeah." Sophia looked at the watch. "You brought it back. I thought of a lot of ways this plan could backfire. Maybe the thief would think the watch was nice and just keep it. But thieves are too greedy to ignore a payday like that. Or maybe a jeweler would decide to look the other way instead of alerting the authorities. But I never in a million years thought the thief would just walk in the door and give it back to me."

"In fairness, I'm not the thief," Chaplin said. "Tinker is the one who took the watch. I didn't even know until we got to California."

"I think it still counts, Miss Byrd, or whatever you said your name was."

"Penny Chaplin."

"Right. Either way, you should have chosen to keep the watch. I don't know how to deal with the fact you brought it back. I don't know if I should be angry or relieved or... or if this is the exception that proves the rule."

Chaplin wrinkled her nose. "I never understood that expression. How can any exception prove a rule?"

"That's really not the issue right now."

"Sure," Chaplin said. "I'm just rambling."

Sophia walked to the other side of the dinner table. She pulled out her chair and sat down, staring at Chaplin the entire time.

"So you really did have to leave town unexpectedly?"

"We really did. There's a guy we pissed off a while back, and Tinker discovered he was coming to town. He's here now, actually."

Sophia frowned. "Wait, is he part of the revival?"

"The reverend. Rumble Riggs."

"You're kidding. I suppose that does make some kind of sense. I've always wanted to take down one of those big fucking tents, but I was too scared. Too big for me to take on by myself." She tapped the table with her fingernail. "You wanted to stay. And you didn't want to steal the watch."

Chaplin nodded. "You have no reason to believe me, but it's the truth. I wanted to tell you what it was worth. I thought the money would be a godsend to you."

"It would help a lot," Sophia admitted. "But like I said, the thrill was more cathartic after what those asses did to my mother."

"Were you at least able to make them pay?"

Sophia shook her head. "I never knew who they were. And they were long gone by the time I got here. So I assume I'll never know for sure. I was content to just take down as many con artists as possible. You'd be surprised how many are roaming around the country."

Chaplin said, "Actually I wouldn't. We run into each other all the time."

"Maybe you could help me find the people who ruined my mother."

"Maybe," Chaplin said. "I'd be happy to try."

Sophia quietly considered everything they'd said. She lifted her head and leaned back to look out the window toward the truck.

"Where is... what did you say her name is? Trucker?"

"Tinker. She... I don't know. She said she had something to do. She didn't..." She shook her head. "We saw something this morning. Out in the desert. It shook us both up." She looked around for the radio. "Have you heard anything? About... explosions? An explosion?"

"No. But I haven't been listening to the news. You saw an explosion?"

Chaplin shook her head. "I don't know what we saw. I just hope it didn't make her do anything stupid."

CHAPTER EIGHTEEN

ALBUQUERQUE, NEW MEXICO
Monday July 16, 1945

The sun was just starting to color the hotel room window when Ephraim "Rumble" Riggs first started to wake up. He grunted, coughed, rolled onto his back, and pulled the thin blanket up over his bulk.

Tinker waited until he had settled into his new position before she stuck her foot out and kicked the bedframe. Riggs snorted in his sleep, his arms and legs jerking as if she'd physically shaken him. He sat up and reached for the nightstand in the same movement, groping for either the lamp or the gun he had in the drawer. Tinker watched as he fumbled around, squinting in the dim light. Maybe he was reaching for his glasses. Whatever his intention, he stopped reaching when he realized who his guest was.

"You. Osker said you slipped through their fingers."

"Osker lied. I tricked him and he felt stupid, so he made up a story. You should definitely hold him accountable for that."

Riggs sneered at her. He looked at the man sitting in the chair next to Tinker. "Who the hell is that?"

Tinker looked at the man as if she'd forgotten he was there. "Oh. Don't worry about him. He's just my guest."

"How did you get in here?"

"You sleep way too deeply," Tinker said. "The gun that was in your drawer is with my friend here. His name is Anthony, by the way. Say hello to the reverend, Anthony."

"Hello," Anthony said.

Riggs glared at the man.

"Your eyeglasses are in my pocket. I don't know why I took them. I thought it would be funny to have you all blurry-eyed. And it's only fair. I've been driving for pretty much an entire day. My eyes feel like sandpaper. So I wanted to even the field a little."

Riggs sat up fully. "Okay. You got away from my men, and now what...? You decided to come back and gloat? Do you really think you'll get out of this hotel in one piece? If I shouted right now, Osker and Vernon and a half-dozen others would fill the hallway up. You wouldn't even get to the stairs before they had you."

"I got to thinking, after I left Osker and Vernon running home with their tails between their legs. I could keep running. I could keep outsmarting you every time our paths cross. But that sounds so exhausting. I'm already tired of it. But the only alternatives are giving up or taking you out. I don't think I'm impressive enough to take down an ape like you. And I don't like the idea of giving up. So I racked my brain and tried to figure out a new angle. And then I thought of something that would work for both of us." She leaned forward. "We could join forces."

Riggs laughed. "You have nothing to offer me."

"Don't I?" Tinker shrugged. "Think about it. Chaplin and I humiliated you twice. We destroyed your revival when we proved you were just a con man. You had to leech onto this one to keep the game going. You sent your best man after me, and even he failed. If I hadn't come back, you might never have seen me again. I could be a huge benefit to your crew. You could hang around longer, do more elaborate cons. Make a lot more money."

Riggs looked intrigued despite himself. "And you'd just abandon your little pal? Chaplin?"

Tinker winced and looked away. "Chaplin is dead."

"What?" Riggs sat up straighter in the bed. "What do you mean dead?"

"You saw in Santa Fe," she said. "I was by myself. Chaplin... Chaplin's gone. And I decided I don't want to do this alone. It's no fun when there's no one to celebrate with, to plan with. And if we're going to keep butting heads, then we might as well make the best of it."

Riggs watched her carefully, or as carefully as he could without his glasses on. "Your father might not be too enthused about bringing you into the fold."

"Who cares what that old man thinks?" Tinker said. "Send the walking corpse back to Texas where he belongs, tell him you made a mistake. I don't give a shit what you tell him. You and I could be good, Riggs. We could make a fortune bilking these suckers out of their money. You wouldn't have to keep looking over your shoulder for me~"

"I never had to look over my shoulder for you. I am not~"

"I destroyed your sham of a church," Tinker interrupted. She stood up and leaned toward Riggs, raising her voice. "I humiliated you in front of your people, and your potential victims. I *ruined* you so badly that you jumped at the chance to get your revenge on me. The only reason you didn't shoot me on the spot is because you wanted me to lead you to Chaplin so you could deal with both of us at once. You can deny it all day, but the truth is, we terrified you. I'm giving you a chance to relax and focus on conning people."

Riggs narrowed his eyes at her. "You wouldn't be an equal. You would be minor league at best. You'd be outranked by everyone. Including Vernon."

"Fine."

"Your cut would be abysmal until you earned equity."

"That's fair enough."

Riggs said, "And the lowest man on the totem pole is the sacrificial lamb. If the cops end up on our trail, you're the one we cut loose to make them scramble."

Tinker shrugged. "Again, seems fair." She looked at Anthony, who had been sitting quietly for the entire conversation. "Is that enough?"

"It's not exactly a smoking gun," Anthony said, standing up and moving to the window. "But compared with the other shit we've gathered on his 'church' over the years, I would say it amounts to a confession." He opened the curtain, pushed up the pane, and stuck his hand outside. He signaled to someone in the street and turned back to the room. "I owe you an apology, Miss Driscoll. I had absolutely no faith that would actually work."

"What?" Riggs said.

Anthony smiled. "We weren't properly introduced, Mr. Riggs. My name is Anthony Stettler. I'm an agent with the Federal Bureau of Investigation. We've been following you and your people for quite a while now. I couldn't believe my luck when Miss Driscoll here walked into our offices this morning at the crack of dawn and said she could get you to confess."

Riggs' face was bright red, his eyes wide enough to bug out. A commotion was starting to rise out in the hallway, shouting and doors slamming open and scuffles between people trying to get past the feds.

"You..." He jabbed a finger at Tinker. "Do you know who she is? *What* she is? She's~"

"A confidence artist," Anthony said, looking at Tinker with something like respect. "Yes, sir. She confessed to that as well. We're going to be taking her into custody as well. But we might be willing to take into consideration how much help she's provided. You're a very big fish, 'Reverend.' We're very happy with her right now. We like to do favors for people we're happy with. But you? You've been a pain in our butts for years now. We are not happy with you or your friends at all."

Riggs scrambled to get out of bed. By the time he was standing, Anthony had a gun casually aimed at his chest.

"You threatened this young woman with a hallway full of 'goons.' You're facing the same problem, friend. Might as well just save everyone some time and trouble and give up now."

Riggs bared his teeth at Tinker. "You are a dead woman."

"Sure," Anthony said. "Keep threatening her in front of a federal agent. That seems like a smart move."

Tinker saw the fight go out of Riggs. His shoulders sagged and his chin dropped. He might have been a giant, but he suddenly looked very small in his sleep shirt and long underwear. He bent his elbows and put his bear-paw hands up with the palms out.

Anthony smiled. "Now that *is* a smart move. Ephraim 'Rumble' Riggs, it gives me great pleasure to officially place you under arrest. Turn around and face the wall, please."

Tinker walked to the hotel room door where two other agents were waiting. They moved to block her from leaving the room, but she stopped and held out her arms with her wrists together.

"Go ahead. We had an agreement."

One agent took the handcuffs from his pocket and stepped forward to officially take her into custody. As he was fastening the bracelets behind her, two agents walked past the room with her father. He was limping, hopefully because the hole she'd shot in his foot never healed right, and he looked every minute of his seventy-plus years. His hair was thin and greasy, hanging over a forehead that looked swollen and misshapen. The agents hadn't let him get dressed, so he was wearing an old white V-neck shirt and striped pajama bottoms.

He glanced over and saw her, rage flashing in his eyes once he recognized her. Tinker smiled at him and lifted her chin in greeting.

"Hey, Dad. I guess you were right when you said I'd be finished if you ever saw my face again." She winked. "Glad I could take you down with me."

The agents dragged him on before he could manage a reply.

Riggs was led out next, requiring four agents to form a fence around his bulk as he was escorted to the stairs.

Anthony waited until he was gone before he approached Tinker. "I asked around before we got to the hotel," he said. "No one has heard anything about any explosions, either in the desert or anywhere else in the country. I got a fair amount of odd looks asking about it." He narrowed his eyes at her. "Did you hear about something? A threat, maybe?"

Tinker shook her head. "No. The more I think about it, the more it seems like it was probably just a sign from the universe."

Anthony shrugged. "Well, whatever it was, we owe it a debt. The streets of this country are a lot safer with Riggs... and, my apologies, you... off of them."

"No offense taken," Tinker assured him. "I made my choice."

He nodded and motioned for the agents to take her out.

She hadn't made her decision to make the country's streets safer. There was only one resident she cared about, and she hoped against hope that she took the opening Tinker had just given her and ran like hell with it.

Sophia decided she wasn't going in to work that day. She was too confused and conflicted about what to do with the con artist who had just dropped into her kitchen. She called the bank to let her boss know she had "fallen sick" and wouldn't be in. Chaplin waved a hand to get her attention and mimed an explosion with her hands.

"Oh. And, um... I have a strange question. Have you heard about anything happening outside of town? Or any kind of big news, I supp~ oh, really?" She frowned as she listened to her boss. "Well, isn't that peculiar..." She chewed her lip and raised an eyebrow. "Well, I'll be. Okay. Yes, thank you. No, I just... something strange woke me up, that's all. Okay. Thank you, Bill. I will. Have a good day."

She hung up and turned to the window.

"Well?" Chaplin asked.

"There are a couple of big stories, apparently," Sophia said. "First, there's an air force base out there somewhere and they told the press that a building full of ammunition blew up. That's probably what you saw."

Chaplin shook her head. "That's bullshit. What I saw was one explosion, not a whole bunch of little ones. An ammunition warehouse would've been like fireworks."

"I suppose we shouldn't be surprised they're lying," Sophia said. "Apparently this town is full of liars. The military is the least surprising liar in the bunch."

Chaplin decided there was no point in pursuing the explosion story any further. Once the military had given their version of events, she might as well try getting water from a stone.

"You said there were other news stories?"

"Yes," Sophia said carefully. "Apparently the Federal Bureau of Investigation did a big bust at the Hotel Albuquerque this morning. Reverend Riggs and most of his employees were taken into custody on charges of theft, forgery, and fraud."

Chaplin stood up. Her heart pounded, and suddenly her hands were tingling. "The feds? They arrested him?"

"And a bunch of other people," Sophia said. "My manager didn't know many details, just that the reverend was put in the back of a black car. He's kind of hard to miss."

Chaplin went to the window, certain she would see police surrounding the house. Instead she saw an empty yard and a quiet street. Her eyes drifted to the car Tinker had given her. "Shit. Tinker did this."

"You can't be sure about that."

"I'm sure," she said. "Given how she was talking this morning... That's why she took the truck. It's why she gave me our entire bankroll. She was cutting me loose to take the fall herself."

Sophia stared, then shook her head. "God. First you bring the watch back, then your partner sacrifices herself to save you. You two might be the worst grifters I've ever seen."

Chaplin turned to look at her, then chuckled. A second later, it turned into a full laugh, and soon she had to lean against the wall to keep from falling over. Sophia laughed as well, even though her eyes betrayed the concern she felt.

"What's so funny?" she finally asked.

"I don't know." Chaplin wiped her eyes. "A couple of hours ago, I thought I was seeing the end of the world. And now, here it is. Just a few hours late."

"And that's funny?" Sophia said.

"No." Chaplin sighed. She wrapped her arms around herself, closed her eyes, and rested her head against the wall. "But laughing is easier."

Chapter Nineteen

ALBUQUERQUE, NEW MEXICO
Friday July 27, 1945

Tinker knew who she would be seeing when the sheriff came to get her. She'd been a guest of the Albuquerque Sheriff's Department for the past two weeks, since there was no women's facility close enough to ship her to. Riggs, her father, and all the revival crew had been shipped out to the penitentiary days ago, but the sheriff had little to no idea what to do with her until the feds came back and told them where she was supposed to go.

The first two days, they'd let her keep the clothes she was wearing when she was taken into custody. After that, she was loaned clothes from the wives and girlfriends of the Albuquerque police force. Today she was wearing a white button-down blouse and slacks that were just a little too tight, a necessity since she wasn't allowed a belt. Her hair was tied back out of her face, a style she'd rarely if ever worn unless she was playing a character. But now that she was entering a new chapter, she decided it was time to try new things and see how they felt.

She stepped into the interrogation room and the door was closed behind her. She glanced at the window as she pulled out the chair. Confident no one in the bullpen was watching, she sat down and focused her angry gaze on the woman on the other side of the table.

"You better have a damn good reason to be sitting there, after everything I sacrificed for you."

Chaplin leaned forward. "Did you think I would just walk away? After everything we've been through together, you thought that conversation by the side of the road was the end?"

Tinker shrugged. "It seemed kind of final."

Chaplin glared at her.

"How'd you manage to get in here to see me?"

She gestured at her suit. "I'm a paralegal at a law firm that is very interested in representing you at trial. Pro bono. Our partners believe everyone has the right to a fair trial, even scum-sucking con artists like yourself. They were very impressed with the fact you did the right thing and took down someone even bigger than yourself, and for that they wanted to reward you."

"Well, isn't that nice of them. And that suit... Sophia?"

"Yeah. I've been staying in the guest house." She adjusted the lapels and ignored Tinker's raised eyebrow. She wasn't going to expand on that in the limited time they had together. "I just needed to talk to you. To understand why you did it."

"Isn't it obvious?"

"No. Well, maybe. I just wanted you to explain it to me. Please."

Tinker sighed and settled back in her chair. "I've always known there are two ways out of this lifestyle. A jail cell or a slab. I always assumed I would end up the way Laffite did. Standing by that road, seeing the... whatever it was. It made me realize the end could come at any second. And the only way I could avoid it was accepting it. Making it work for me." She shrugged. "This way, I get to stop Riggs and save you at the same time. I consider that a pretty fair trade-off for a few years of freedom."

Chaplin clenched her jaw. "But where does that leave me? What am I supposed to do, huh?"

"Well, Laffite always thought there was a cycle. You know? She taught me everything she knew, then cut me loose. I found you, we made a good team for a while, and now..." She gestured across the table. "What happens next is up to you. But if I can make a suggestion? Just one last piece of advice?"

"Sure, why not."

"Don't find a new partner. Break the cycle. It's a fun ride for a while, but it always ends in tragedy. There's no happy ending here. Look at us. I love you, and we still nearly ended up coming to blows because of this dumb job. You have a big nest egg. You can live comfortably anywhere you want until you figure out something legitimate."

"Yeah," Chaplin laughed. "I'll get a paper route or something."

"I'm serious. You're smart and you're a quick learner. You'll find a way to survive. To live a real life, not this drifting and grifting. You have more of an opportunity than I ever did, with Sophia. Focus on what you have there. I think it'll be worth the effort."

Chaplin chewed her bottom lip and looked around the small interrogation room.

"And you just go to prison?"

"Like I said, I was heading there anyway. This way it's on my own terms, and I get the rewards I choose. I'm not complaining. I do regret taking your truck away, but I think you'll figure out a way over that hurdle."

Chaplin looked down at her hands. "I love you too, you know. Just~"

"Not in the way I love you." She chuckled. "Yeah. I know. Unrequited love is only tragic if it's wasted. Doing this, saving you... that's how I show my love for you."

Chaplin blinked back tears. "And I just take it? I don't get a chance to repay the favor?"

Tinker laughed. "How? Are you going to blast down the wall and bust me out of here?" She shook her head. "No. It's a gift. I'm satisfied with my road ending here. If you want to pay me back, make it worthwhile. Don't become another nameless, penniless con artist stabbed to death on a train."

"You knew about how Lafitte died."

"Yeah." Tinker's voice was rough. "I knew. Promise me."

"I promise."

"Good girl." Tinker held her hand out. Chaplin stared at it, then put her own on top of it, curled her fingers around it. "You know, a lot of grifters and cons lie to themselves about the end of their careers. They ignore the inevitable and insist they'll be the ones who win the game. They'll hit one big score and get out while the going is good."

Chaplin nodded. "That's what *I* was planning to do."

"Yeah?" Tinker said. "Then *do it*. The score is that woman you're staying with. She looks at you the way you deserve to be looked at. And you look at her the way I wish you'd look at me. I pulled you away from her because I was jealous. That was wrong. You need to hold onto her tight. Don't let anyone tear you away from her, and don't abandon her just to go chasing after some potential high. This life you're looking at right now? That's the big score. And it's yours for the taking."

"I don't know if I even know how to live like that. A quiet, normal life."

Tinker smiled. "You've always been great at slipping into a new character's skin. Just tell yourself it's part of a long con. Before you know it, it'll just be muscle memory."

"And what about you?"

"Prison. Probably a lot of prison. Decades of crimes across state lines, and I've pretty much confessed to everything, so the trial won't be much more than a formality. As for you..." She leaned forward and lowered her voice. "Penny Chaplin is dead. They won't be looking for her, so make sure they don't stumble over you by accident. Understand?"

"I understand."

"That means no more visits."

Chaplin nodded. "I understand."

Tinker smiled and a tear slipped free, rolling down her cheek. "It's great to see you, though. One last time."

"Take care of yourself, Tinker."

"Oh, I'm going by Emilie now." She shrugged. "I figured I might as well lay Tinker to rest."

Chaplin nodded. "Goodbye, Emilie."

"Goodbye, Penny. Go get your reward."

Chaplin stood up and wiped her eyes before she knocked on the door to be let out. She turned to look back at Emilie.

"You saved my life. You *made* it a life. I'll never forget that."

Emilie nodded. "You saved mine, too. I never would've done this for anyone else. So thank you, Penny. Thank you for giving me an ending I can be proud of."

The door opened and a deputy stepped to the side to let Chaplin out. She stared at Emilie for a moment longer, as if she was burning the image of her into her mind.

Then she turned and left without looking back.

Chaplin took down her hair as she walked from the driveway to the house. For the past two weeks, they had been acting the roles of landlady and tenant. Sophia still invited Chaplin to the main house for dinner most nights, and sometimes Chaplin played the piano for her. But they didn't touch unless they had to. They definitely didn't share a bed. It was almost like their first night together hadn't happened.

On the whole, Chaplin was glad for that. They had moved too fast, and they'd almost had the rug yanked out from under them. This time, this unusual gap between the life she knew and whatever lay ahead, was a gift. They were taking the chance to get to know each other. She was earning Sophia's trust honestly, building a true connection instead of one built on a lie. Sophia, for her part, seemed willing to forgive Chaplin for the lies given how things had ended up, but she knew forgiveness was still a fair distance away.

Sophia was waiting in the living room and stood up when she came in. "How was she?"

"I don't know," Chaplin said. "She seemed fine, but I don't..." She chuckled and shook her head. "After all these years, I'm still not entirely sure when she's lying to me. But I think she made her choice. She's accepted whatever happens to her as long as it means I get to go free."

Sophia stopped in front of Chaplin. "And how do *you* feel about her sacrificing herself that way? She didn't exactly give you a choice in the matter."

"No. And I would have said absolutely not if she had asked. But the damage is done, so the only thing I can do is be grateful." She put her hands on Sophia's shoulders and looked into her eyes. "She said the only time unrequited love is tragic is when it's wasted. It would be wasteful if I kept putting myself in danger. Either physically or with the law. So I'm... I'm going to stop. I'm going to have a nice, legal life. It doesn't have to be here, or with you. I'd like it to be. But I don't want to put any pressure on~"

Sophia cupped Chaplin's face and kissed her, stopping the rant before it could begin. She leaned into the kiss, moved her hands down to Sophia's waist, and stepped in to close the distance between them. She'd been dreaming of another kiss since their night together, but she had accepted the fact it might be a long time before they were at the right place again.

Now she parted her lips against Sophia's and felt her respond. She moaned quietly and put one hand in the small of Sophia's back, just above her belt, and deepened the kiss.

When Sophia pulled away, Chaplin dropped her hand. She

took a step back and blinked. She had to clear her head of all the feelings the kiss had stirred up.

"Give me back my suit," Sophia said.

Chaplin was confused. "I was going to. I was going to wash~"

"Penny," Sophia interrupted. She reached out and started unbuttoning the jacket. "Give me... back... my suit. Right now."

"Oh." Chaplin let Sophia brush the jacket off her shoulders, then stepped in for another kiss. The jacket fell to the floor, and Sophia went to work on the buttons as she started to back away, holding the kiss as she used the blouse to pull Chaplin toward the bedroom.

Sophia stopped at the doorway of the bedroom. Chaplin was in her bra, her slacks undone, her hair mussed from Sophia running her fingers through it.

"This doesn't mean everything is fine now," she said. "It doesn't mean all is forgiven, it doesn't mean I'm over all the bad things you've done."

"I know," Chaplin said.

"You do?"

Chaplin nodded and brushed Sophia's cheek. "Yeah. This is just where we start."

Sophia searched Chaplin's face for signs of betrayal or deception. Then, releasing a quiet sigh of surrender, and pulled Chaplin to her and walked her into the bedroom.

Epilogue

CALIFORNIA INSTITUTION FOR WOMEN
Tehachapi, California
Monday September 18, 1950

Five years after surrendering herself to the Albuquerque sheriff, Emilie Driscoll walked out of prison and into a completely new world. It was a new decade. The world war had ended and a new one had apparently started, some aggression over in Korea. Her hair was unfashionably short and, equally unfashionably, now completely silver-gray. Her cellmate, a lovely woman named Stephanie, insisted it made her look like she was wearing a crown. Emilie didn't argue that crowns were gold, not silver, and accepted the compliment.

A week before she was due to be released, a package arrived addressed to Emilie T. Driscoll. She didn't have a middle name, but the initial was more than enough for her to know who sent it. Inside was a journal detailing the time she and Chaplin had spent together. All the grifts and cons they'd pulled across the country from Chaplin's point of view. Emilie read through a full year before she realized the journal was Chaplin's own confession. But this was intended for Sophia, not the police. Chaplin was owning up to the crimes she'd committed and the victims she'd left in her wake. She was taking responsibility for the damage they'd caused over the five years they'd spent as partners.

The journal ended on the day they saw the Trinity explosion. Emilie sometimes still questioned whether that had been real or just a shared hallucination. Yes, they now had official confirmation of what was happening in the desert a hundred miles south of Albuquerque. But it had been such a perfect, undeniable omen that she wanted to believe it really was a sign meant for the two of them.

The package also contained a bus ticket that would take her three hundred miles north to Sacramento, where she assumed she was supposed to proceed to the address written on the last page of the journal. She debated ignoring the tacit invitation and giving the ticket to another inmate being released on the same day. Five years was a long time, and it felt like an invasion to just walk back into Chaplin's life after so long.

In the end, she decided she had nowhere else to go. There was no reason to run and hide. Her father had died within six months of his arrest, after trying to con another inmate who was smarter and meaner than he was. And Riggs was convicted on so many counts that he wasn't leaving prison unless it was in a coroner's bag. So she took the bag of meager possessions she'd had with her when she was sent to prison and boarded the bus.

Most of the day passed on the bus. She ate a sandwich that she picked up at one of their stops, napped, and read a newspaper someone had left behind from the front page to the classifieds. Mostly she just watched the world roll by outside the window. It felt strange to be traveling such a massive distance after five years in a cell. She'd almost forgotten what it was like to cover hundreds of miles like this. She also thought it was ironic she finally made it to California after all.

By the time the bus arrived at the Sacramento station, she was bone-weary. It was dinner time, and she considered putting off the reunion until morning. She could find somewhere to stay, get something proper to eat, change out of her dingy old clothes... But the draw of seeing Chaplin again was too great. She found a taxicab and handed the address to the driver.

Ten minutes later, she instructed him to leave her at the end of the street. He pointed out the right direction as she paid him. She had transferred her things into a bag with a shoulder strap, so she slung it on and strolled down the street in the dying light.

The neighborhood was quaint, with row upon row of gorgeous

little houses hidden behind shrubs, trees, and short fences. The windows glowed with soft yellow light. They looked like homes. The kind of home she'd never let herself hope for, but now felt a certain longing to have for herself. She smiled at the thought of Chaplin ending up here.

The address was in the middle of the street. There was a car parked at the curb, and the lawn was encircled by a wooden fence. A neatly-tended and vibrant flower bed stood at the edge of the front porch. Emilie stood at the gate and smiled up at the house for a long moment before she continued on. She knocked and took a step back, head down, wondering what she could say when the door opened. A week of planning and eight hours on the road, and she hadn't given a single thought about what she'd actually say when she got here.

The porch light switched on and the door opened. Chaplin's hair was cut short, center-parted so that it hung down in two wildly curly waves. Her glasses were much too big but still somehow managed to fit her face perfectly. She wore a pale green blouse and tan slacks. She was tanned, but not so much that it obscured her freckles. She laughed, put a hand over her mouth, and then stepped over the threshold to wrap her arms around Emilie in a tight hug.

"Hello," Chaplin said against Emilie's shoulder.

Emilie returned the hug tentatively at first, but then she squeezed tighter. "Hello, Penny."

Chaplin took a step back. Her eyes were wide and shining. "Look at you."

"Look at *you*," Emilie said. "Domestic life, huh?"

Chaplin laughed and looked down at herself. "Wow. How did this happen?" She swept her hair away from her face. "So you're out?"

"I'm out," Emilie said.

Sophia came into the hall, wiping her hands on a towel. Her hair was longer, and paler blonde than Emilie remembered, but her eyebrows were as thick and dark as ever.

"Yes, she's out," Sophia said, "and a proper hostess would have invited her to come inside and join us for dinner instead of just standing out on the porch."

"Shoot, yes." Chaplin stepped aside and ushered Emilie in. "Come on inside, come on."

Emilie came into the house and slipped the bag off her shoulder. She looked at Sophia and awkwardly shifted her weight from one foot to the other.

"We haven't been properly introduced. I'm Emilie Driscoll."

Sophia smiled and held out her now-dry hand. "Hello, Emilie. Sophia. And I believe you know my partner..." She gestured at Chaplin, who had closed the door and come to join them.

"Refresh my memory?" Emilie said.

Chaplin grinned. "Samantha Knox." She shrugged. "I've always liked the name Samantha."

"It suits you. And Knox...?"

"It was one of the available names, when I got my new papers," Samantha explained. "I liked how it sounded. Like opportunity knocking."

Sophia smiled, "And it's where the keep the gold."

Emilie grinned. "It's good. I like it. So... Emilie and Samantha. It could take some getting used to."

Sophia said, "Well, take as long as you need. We have a guest room, and you're more than welcome to it until you know what your next step is."

"Really?" Emilie was genuinely surprised. "I didn't expect to set up camp here."

"Of course." Sophia stepped forward and put her arm around Samantha's waist. "This woman is the best thing that's ever happened to me. She saved me from spiraling into a cycle of revenge that probably would have eventually gotten me killed. And she would never have come into my life if it wasn't for you."

"Not to mention the fact I owe you for protecting me when you took down Riggs," Samantha said. "You didn't have to do that."

Emilie said, "Yes, I did. It was... it was the right call. And I would do it again in a heartbeat."

Sophia nodded. "So letting you have the spare room is a small price to pay for our partnership and Sam's freedom. We won't take no for an answer."

"Then I won't waste energy fighting you."

Sophia nodded. "Sam said you were smart." She turned to Samantha and kissed her cheek. "Show her where she can wash up? I'm going to go finish up with dinner."

Samantha nodded and watched her partner go, then gestured for Emilie to follow her. They walked down a short hall to a bathroom that was decorated in pale beige, light blue, and two dozen seashells. Emilie blinked as she stepped over the threshold, trying to take it all in.

"Wow," she said.

"Yeah," Samantha laughed and leaned against the door frame. "She missed Albuquerque when we moved, and beach theme is more inviting than a desert, so. It was a compromise.

Emilie looked at her, impressed. "You really have gone domestic, haven't you?"

"Don't knock it."

"I'm not." Emilie turned on the tap and washed her hands. "If anything, I'm jealous. Long way from sleeping in the truck, huh."

Samantha whistled and shook her head. "It feels like a whole other life."

"It was," Emilie said. "Penny Chaplin's life. And Tinker's. Those women never left the desert. I like to think they'd be happy to see what we've done with ourselves."

"Oh, they are. Definitely. Towels are under the sink."

Emilie retrieved one and dried her hands. She looked at herself in the mirror, and Samantha stepped into the room to join her.

"So what's the next step, hm?" Emilie asked.

"Life." Samantha put a hand on Emilie's shoulder. "In the big picture, at least. In the smaller frame, my wife made us a very delicious dinner, and she gets cross if I'm late to the table."

"Can't have the missus getting angry."

Samantha smiled and left the bathroom.

Emilie gave her reflection one last look. She didn't know what life meant, at least not at this stage. But she had a safe place to figure it out, and Cha~ Samantha had a head start on adjusting to normality. She could show Emilie the ropes, the same way Tinker had shown Chaplin how to live a life on the road. The idea of coming full circle like that very much appealed to her.

"If you don't hurry up," Sophia called, "we're going to start without you!"

Emilie laughed. "Coming."

She turned out the lights and went to join her friends for dinner.

Geonn Cannon is the author of over sixty novels, including the Riley Parra series which was adapted into an Emmy-nominated webseries by Tello Films. His novel *Can You Hear Me* was adapted into *Static Space*, an award-winning short film. He's also written two tie-in novels for the television series *Stargate SG-1*. He was the first male author to win a Golden Crown Literary Society Award for his novel *Gemini*, and he won a second for *Dogs of War*.